EXEUNT

A novel by Ralph Bland

ISBN

Published by dpdotcom publishing

Exeunt

"I suppose it's like the ticking crocodile, isn't it?
Time is chasing after all of us."

J.M. Barrie
Peter Pan

"I been a long time leaving but I'm going to be a long
time gone."
Willie Nelson

"Exit, Stage Left."
Snagglepuss

Exeunt

Abington, Tennessee

(Christmas Day, 1988)

Miller Hill leans back in his faithful old office chair and watches one more in a continuing series of morons bounce off the front door of the store. This particular nincompoop, dressed as he is in a long winter coat with a stocking cap and donning walking shorts in December, doesn't see fit to read the sign posted on the glass in front of his nose that says Overton's Market is closed (even though it is past noon on Christmas Day and not a damn thing else in town is open either), but instead just keeps pushing on the door three or four more times until he is at last convinced it isn't stuck or he is simply not strong enough to open such a portal, finally giving up in frustration and walking back to his car. Miller is not certain if the sign ever did actually get read by this guy or not, but he'll bet the ranch it hadn't, since the majority of the cliental of Overton's Market have never been the most vociferous readers occupying the civilized world. It would be stretching it, he thinks, to believe that very many of them can even decipher words and their definitions at all.

The phone rings and Miller studies the blinking light on the console. He decides to let it flash a while, maybe give it five more times to see if whoever's on the other end of the line is completely serious about calling or not. Probably it is another dumbass wanting to know if the store is open or not, but Miller has to at least give them a little credit for calling first before coming over here to bounce off the door like the rest of the town is choosing to do. Any other time Miller would let this call go unanswered, but he is in a funny and wicked kind of mood this early Christmas afternoon, sort of like he always seems to be these days unless he is passed out or ripped or happily intoxicated or all three in combination, so he picks up the receiver and punches the line button down with his finger. Time for some fun and entertainment, he thinks.

"Overton's," he says. "Merry Christmas," he adds, just for the hell of it.

"I had a feeling you'd be there," a voice says. By all indications this voice sounds like it has recently awakened from a short period of sleep after one hell of a hard night of drinking diesel fuel, so at least Miller knows he is speaking to a familiar and kindred spirit.

"I tried your house but there wasn't any answer." It is Sammy Walker calling, which is no surprise to Miller. Most people like to spend Christmas Day and holidays doing something wholesome like hanging out with their families, but Sammy is like him. Anytime he has to do anything human and ordinary it's never anything but a regular drag and can't be escaped from fast enough. "I figured it was that, or maybe you'd gone over the river and through the trees to Granny's house," Sammy says, "or there was also that possibility you might be laying in your bed dead as a yuletide doornail."

"Dear old Granny's the one who's dead," Miller states, "going on twenty years or so now, so the family as a rule doesn't go over to her house and open presents much anymore. Nothing under the damn tree and Granny just can't seem to get it together to cook any kind of a holiday dinner, which is a shame, since I always delighted in her prune pineapple cakes as a lad. Besides, my folks have gone off deep sea fishing down in Florida somewhere with a bunch of other liberated retirees who are as a group all sick and tired of looking at grandkids and have decided this year to get good and far away from kids for a nice change. Of course, I, being celibate in my practices, have never created a grandchild for my own folks to dote on, so they're free to take off anytime they want for exotic locales. For my own personal Christmas celebration, I figured I'd keep with holiday tradition this one last time and come by the store and check the refrigeration and just, you know, sit here on my ass soaking up the ambience for a while."

"You probably could have let that refrigeration check pass this Christmas. The power could go off and everything go all to shit and what would it matter? Everything will be gone in a week anyway."

"Don't remind me."

Sammy is referring to the fact that by this time next week, Sunday, to be precise, it will be New Year's Day, and by then Overton's Market will be closed down for good, history, lights out for eternity. Come and visit us in our new location, the sign on the front window says. Wider aisles, better selection, open twenty-four hours a day and seven days a week for your shopping convenience. Your brand-new one-stop shopping center, clean, well-lighted, a friendly and courteous staff to wait on you with all the up to date modern varieties you've always wanted right at your fingertips. Welcome to the new state of the art way of grocery shopping in Abington, Tennessee.

"So, what's up today, chief?" Sammy asks. "I don't know what your feelings are about all this holiday stuff, but I'm ready for this Christmas crap to hurry up and be over and done with. I've already had Christmas breakfast this morning here at my mom's and stuffed myself to where I can't walk or even want to think about trying to. My little brother's kids have new bikes and are outside pedaling up and down the street popping wheelies, and Mom and Dad are cleaning up and packing up and getting ready to go to my uncle's place somewhere out in the fucking middle of nowhere to spend the rest of the day, and if I don't get myself up and moving and out of here like pronto they're going to be expecting me to ride out into the wilderness with them, so I've got to get the fuck out of Dodge real soon. Screw all that let's go visit with the relatives because it's Christmas Day bullshit. I had enough of that crap when I was seven years old."

"I do happen to have a little surplus weed we could maybe sample later on," Miller says, "if you're up for something like that. Nothing like being good and ripped for a major holiday, you know. We could get nice and lit-up and go to a movie or something. I don't know what's on, but if I'm buzzed enough I don't really care. I can watch Oral Roberts heal possessed people on television and be pretty entertained."

"We can probably come up with something better than that. I've been thinking about just going all-out and start beseeching God for a little Christmas miracle," Sammy says. "Get my prayer requests all primed and laid out on His to-do list early, because a miracle is about what it's going to take to get me through this next week without losing my goddamn mind."

"If I was you, buddy, I wouldn't count on the Holy Father helping you with your problems anytime soon, because your track record hasn't really warranted too many celestial favors lately. That's just my opinion, though. I could be wrong. Never have been before, but there's a first time for everything."

Miller hangs up. He's glad he remembered to turn the radio off last night when they finally got all the last-second shoppers out and the doors locked, otherwise Christmas music would still be pouring out over the intercom right now and he might be tempted to go ballistic at the sound. He's heard enough of "Winter Wonderland" and "O Little Town of Bethlehem" to carry him over until next year at least, and his holiday spirit—as if he ever had any in the first place—is used up and kaput. It's time to put the holly and gay apparel and everything yuletide that goes with it away. He looks at the wreaths and snowmen and cheery decorations plastered on the office windows and draped over the checkout lanes, all the merry Christmas garbage dangling from the light fixtures and taped on the walls. The entire collection needs to be taken down and boxed up, but it seems like such a wasted effort. It isn't like any of this crap is going to go over to the new store to get used again next year. No, the goddamn new store will have all new decorations, so all this ancient shit he's been looking at for the last twenty years plus now might as well get thrown in the dumpster, get hauled off and buried or burned up or just left here to get bulldozed next week—whatever in the hell gets done with useless junk nobody wants around anymore.

The store is cemetery quiet, like the world is after a deep icy snowfall when nobody can get outside and start making a lot of noise. All he can hear are freezers kicking on and off every now and then back by the meat department and over in the last aisle of the frozen food. He leans back in his chair and the springs make a loud groaning noise in protest, and he half-expects to hear the echo bounce off the walls and careen up and down the empty aisles.

Six more days, he thinks. He's free to start counting them down now, like he's on Death Row and all the appeals are exhausted and his number is up and there's nothing out there in the whole wide world that can save him from meeting his fate.

***

Thank god Dino's is open, because the rest of Abington is shut down tighter than a tick. Christmas coming on a Sunday this year means that most businesses in town will be closed on Monday for the holiday also, so it is like the town's citizens are being given a nice rest, even if the majority of their lazy asses don't deserve one. Working at Overton's over the years, though, has never really given Miller or Sammy too many opportunities to have this sort of respite from routine, because the Market has been open for business every day all that time except for Christmas and Thanksgiving, always staying open until midnight and re-opening early the next morning, the doors seemingly eternally ajar, the days and nights constantly spent weathering one crisis after another, and it has constantly been like it was just the two of them who were the ones there working and taking care of it all, keeping the place from crumbling or falling down in a heap. It was rare when one or both of them didn't have to jump in and solve whatever crisis that was going on. It was like the two of them had taken care of the place a thousand times more than the goddamn Overton family who actually owned the place ever dreamed of doing.

In these last days of 1988 Miller and Sammy are still working at Overton's, twenty-plus years of going in together after high school and college and other wastes of time and money. Their friends grew up working at the Market too, bagging orders and stocking shelves as teenagers, going off to college and working during breaks and summers, but other than Miller and Sammy everyone else has moved on to other things now, like Phillip Ray teaching History fifty miles away at West Tennessee State, or John Chapman working for the electric company up in McGinnis, and David Holbert at Abington Home and Hardware through his recent second marriage which has ended in divorce the same way as his first, which is hard to believe and a real major miracle to everybody, Miller and Sammy and John and Phillip, since none of them have yet to figure out how goddamn David, who they grew up with and know like a book, has managed to get one woman in the world to marry him, much less two. The world never offers valid explanations, they have learned, never has and never will. And women still go parading by them all in continuing shades of mystery. Now that everybody is back in town for the holidays, these are the kinds of subjects they tend to broach, as if there was anything else more important to worry about or discuss.

Some things never change.

"There's something I've never figured out," Sammy says. "If this place is called Dino's, how come the guy who runs it ain't named Dino and is actually from Toronto, hasn't ever been to Italy once in his life, and doesn't have one drop of Italian blood in his whole body? You look at this menu and there isn't one thing on here that's even close to being Italian. You can't get spaghetti or pizza here, so why in the hell is it called Dino's?"

"Maybe he just loves Dean Martin," Phillip says. "Maybe all his life he's secretly yearned to be a member of the Rat Pack. It could be he wants to be like

Sammy and Joey and Frank and have that camaraderie thing going on."

"Sammy Davis Jr. wasn't Italian," Miller counters, "so it can't be a Rat Pack thing."

"I didn't say he was trying to be Italian," Phillip says. "I said maybe he just likes Dean Martin. Back in the day my mother sure did, and she was nothing but pure WASP. She used to commandeer the living room TV and watch The Dean Martin Show every Thursday night. I think secretly she wanted to leave my dad and go run off with Dino and let him sing 'That's Amore' to her the rest of her life."

"My dad always wanted to watch Tennessee Ernie Ford," John says. He takes a sip of beer and moves a fat french fry through a pool of ketchup on his plate. "Heck, deep down inside I think he probably still wants to be Tennessee Ernie. He's probably hoping to be reincarnated as the old pea-picker in his next life as soon as he can hurry up and get this existence he's stuck in over and done with and out of the way."

"My dad was always in love with Dinah Shore," says David. "I could tell it just by watching him. Damn Dinah would come out at the start of the show grinning and singing about seeing the U.S.A. in a Chevrolet and twirling around, and Daddy would just sit there transfixed, like the whole goddamn world had stopped turning and he and Dinah were in some private little place all alone."

"You were an observant little fucker, weren't you?" Sammy asks. "You probably had the hots for her too, even if you only were about seven or so. I ain't surprised, though. You've been a horny little shit as long as I've known you."

"I had to stay on my toes all the time," David grins. "My parents were weird, you know, and if I didn't watch it they'd drag me down into the quicksand with them. My mother was always making me go to church, while my dad kept trying to get me to play football and be a star, even though I weighed about a hundred pounds and everybody else was twice my size. I grew up thinking he wanted me killed and my mother was making sure that when that finally happened I'd at least get to take the sweet chariot ride on up to Heaven."

"My parents never have watched TV together," Miller says. "My dad didn't want to see anything but Jackie Gleason and the Falstaff Game of the Week, and my mother just wanted to go off into another room and read. I grew up watching 'The Twilight Zone' by myself on a little black and white TV back in my room. Sometimes I had to hold the antenna with my fingers to get a clear picture just so I could see Rod Serling."

"Your entire life has pretty much been the twilight zone for a long time," Phillip grins.

"I was wondering if anybody had noticed."

"Hard as hell not to see if you're paying any attention at all."

John sets his mug down on the table and straightens up in his chair. He looks at a couple standing by the doorway searching around for an empty table.

"Well, shit. I sure am glad to see my darling ex-wife is out for a night on the town," he says. He motions toward the door, where a man and a woman stand looking for a place to sit. "If you guys pay close attention I think you can spot the guy she decided to fuck me over for. Handsome goddamn asshole, don't you think? From what I've been told he makes a lot of money too. No wonder dear Carol went shopping for another guy. When it comes to looks and money I never stood a chance."

From their table the five of them look at Carol Nations Chapman and her date or perhaps even her husband by now, who knows for certain, since none of them have seen her or heard anything about her from John much since she and John had divorced two years ago. Everybody sits and waits, hoping maybe she and her current amour will turn around and leave and nobody will have to be a witness to another episode of John Chapman becoming unhinged. Everybody's seen this unpretty transformation thing go down enough times down through the years and none of them really need an encore on this night of the Blessed Child.

"Think I'll go over and say hi," John says cordially, scooting his chair back.

"Here we go," Sammy says. "So much for peace on earth and good will and all that bullshit."

John is on his feet approaching the couple before anybody can get up and stop him. When he gets to them he smiles and shakes the guy's hand and motions back toward the table to Carol so she can see all his old friends sitting there grinning and toothy and friendly-like. She waves and they all wave back.

In a minute John returns to the table, smiling and smoothing his moustache down with his fingers, like he is some circus ringmaster and has just put on the greatest show on earth. He sits down and finishes off his beer and pours another full mug from the pitcher in the center of the table. "Well, that was fun," he says. "The last time I talked to Carol I'm pretty sure I told her I'd kill her new boyfriend if I ever ran across him. That's why I went over and shook his hand and told them both to have a Merry Christmas. Hell, the only thing about it is this dude is not even the same guy I had on my list to kill someday. He's a new one. It's been two long years and in the meantime I forgot what the previous asshole even looked like."

This is not completely the truth, but John feels better saying it anyway. He laughs and holds his beer up to the light, inspecting it for bubbles and color, amazed at how he has been able to transfer all his marital woes and faults over to Carol over the course of a few years, when the truth is he is the one who started fucking up their marriage to begin with. There were a lot of women he couldn't say no to back then and he was dead certain they all wanted him and there hadn't seemed like a whole lot he could do about it except say yes. He had always had this way of not being able to turn his back on stuff like that.

***

They vacate Dino's just after ten, with nowhere really to go or nothing particularly to do but get into David's Dodge Caravan and drive through downtown and see what kind of drama might be taking place around town on this Christmas night, muggings with blood or hookers strung out so bad they can't even take the holiday off, poor souls begging money and guys without homes looking for a place to sleep. There is not much out in the streets they haven't seen before, so they head over to Paradise Pool to play the pinball machines a while, to gamble a little and sober up somewhat, maybe to even get lucky and win a little money.

15

Old Tony begins watching them immediately as they group around the Bally Big Wheel. It seems to Old Tony that every time this particular group comes in one of them seems to win a big payoff on one of the pinballs, and he hasn't figured out how they are doing it yet, not even after watching them about a thousand times over the years. He knows they're doing something tricky, though. He's been around pinball machines and pool halls and such all his life, and he knows nobody stays lucky all the time.

The best pinball player of the group is Phillip, who somehow has always been the one of them able to remain cool and collected and not go nuts when he loses, but who simply chalks it up as a business expense and adopts a new winning strategy with the next quarter he drops in the slot. Phillip has been like this since back in high school, when everybody first started coming into Paradise Pool. Sammy was the one who'd been donating his money to the pinball machines for a while by then, but it had been Phillip who had advanced quickly to the head of the class. Phillip could juke and lean and snake with the best of them, like he was innately born with the talent. Somebody else might get on a hot streak and win money every now and then, but it was Phillip who generally walked out the door with more than he'd walked in with. Even on his bad nights, when he'd play for hours trying to make headway, he usually went home with a profit. It was this way from the start. Phillip was a natural born pinball ace. Not so with everyone else. For everyone else, sometimes the only way to not leave Paradise Pool broke with a deep hole in the gut of your very soul was to come up with a way to defy the odds.

In other words, to cheat.

Old Tony, the head of the Greek family that owns Paradise Pool, is ancient and has been that way for quite a while. Old Tony is the father of Middle Tony, who is up there in years himself, and the grandfather of Young Tony, who is still ten years older than any of them are. Old Tony has it in his head that he still runs Paradise Pool, although Middle Tony had been the one in charge of the hall even from the first time they'd begun coming in, which has been a while back now, twenty years at least, but Old Tony still roams around the room watching all the action going on with a suspicious eye. He can't really see anything clearly and hasn't been able to for a long time, but he spends his time diligently watching anyway for what he imagines in his head just might be illicitly going on. There is a speaker above the Big Wheel and the Beach Boys sing "Kokomo" from an island somewhere far removed from Christmas night here at Paradise Pool. Sammy and John walk off to play Snooker while Miller and David crowd around the Big Wheel to watch Phillip do his thing. Phillip has this way of setting his palms on each corner of the machine and sliding his abdomen into the middle portion of the metal panel, almost as if the Big Wheel is a woman waiting for him to do the dirty deed with her. He pulls the knob and springs the silver ball into action and taps each side of the machine to make it change direction, to slow it down or speed it up, to roll past one hole and settle into the numbered slot he's highlighted up on the screen. Phillip, even with moving away some years ago and not having any practice for long periods of time, is still damn good at this, like he is a mallard and this is a pond. Everyone would still bet a huge amount of dough that Phillip can make the silver ball of the Big Wheel sit up and beg anytime he wants it to. Miller and David watch Phillip press the reset button and see the ball pop up and spring forward, each time marveling at the control Phillip has over the speed and direction it takes. None of them can play the Big Wheel like Phillip can, nobody they know of either, but even as good as Phillip is the damn Wheel is still a tough opponent and is always hard to beat. The Wheel is there to take your money--Paradise Pool doesn't keep the Big Wheel around to pay money out and not make a profit. The object of having the Wheel around is to deplete the wallet of the person who's playing it, get him addicted, tease him a little, and then bring him back the next night to do it all over again. If he wins enough once or twice to keep him coming back and then finally loses what he'd won the nights before, that was fine. That was dandy. But this business of somebody walking in and winning every single time they play is never supposed to happen.

Miller leans back against the wall and watches Phillip go at it. He wonders how Phillip ever got this good. He remembers the one and only time that he himself won any money off the Big Wheel. It was four dollars. It was nothing, but to Miller it had been the accomplishment of a lifetime. He'd collected his four dollars and decided at the same time he would never play the Wheel again. He would quit as a winner after losing his pants for so long. There might be another pinball he'd play now and then, but the Big Wheel would never suck him dry and break his heart again. And unlike most of the vows he'd made in his life, he'd managed to keep this one so far. He's so serious about this promise he keeps his distance, concentrates on keeping a few paces back from the Big Wheel's proximity lest he gets sucked in.

"Need a one, six, or seven," Phillip mutters. He has always talked to himself when he plays the Big Wheel.

"Don't need a nine whatsoever. Nothing on the third row." David, being cheap, never has played any of the machines at Paradise Pool. He'll play a few games of pool every now and then if he's bored, but he's not good enough to ever win, so he for sure won't play for money. He's cheap. The other reason is he knows he is never able to stop the guys from messing with him when he joins in. About a thousand years back he'd played Rotation with everybody and Sammy had dropped a cigarette butt into his Pepsi while he wasn't looking, and when he'd taken a big swig from the bottle everybody had died laughing and hooted and screeched like it was the funniest thing they'd ever seen, practically rolling on the goddamn floor rubbing it in for the next hour. Somebody still always asks him if he'd like a butt with that drink he's having. They're real screams, these friends of his. He buys a can from the machine in the corner and sips on it and watches Phillip work out on the Big Wheel, all the while keeping his finger over the opening of the can so nobody can drop anything in there while he isn't looking. John is all the way over by the far wall playing Snooker with Sammy, but he can hear the clicking sound coming from the direction of the Wheel and he knows what's going on. He'd have to be dead not to know. He's moved away to McGinnis a couple of years now and only makes it back to town three or four times a year, but he's heard this sound so many times before in the past it's impossible to not know what it is.

After four games coming up a loser and with closing time only a few minutes away, Phillip and Miller have reverted to their old trick of making Old Tony believe Phillip has hit a winning game. Since Old Tony is close to blind it is pretty much impossible for him to see the numbers displayed up on the Big

Wheel's board, so Phillip points at the counter and tells Old Tony what is there, a total which actually isn't what he says. Young Tony is off because it is Christmas and he has girlfriends to see and plow, and Middle Tony is at the far end of the hall talking to another group of men, who are laughing at his dirty jokes and listening to his tales about a character called The Bandit. Even all the way at the front of the hall they can hear Middle Tony reminding everyone present to do what he has always advised them to do, which is to eat shit and bark at the moon. You can be gone and live in another town for a while if you want, but when you come back you always discover how nothing much ever changes at Paradise Pool.

"One sixty, Tony," Phillips says, pointing up to the Wheel's counter, which actually reads sixty. "That makes eight bucks you owe me."

"I don't see nothing up there," Old Tony says. He is hunched over the Big Wheel attempting to get close enough to see what is says on the counter. He doesn't want to admit he is too blind to make the numbers out. "I'm resetting it for you, Tony," Miller says. He starts tapping on the side with his car keys like the machine is clicking off the numbers back to zero, but he doesn't actually push the button to reset the score to zero, so Phillip can keep his sixty points up there and add them on to the next game and win again. This is the trick they've been playing on Old Tony for years. Old Tony knows something is going on that is not right and hasn't been for quite a while, but he hasn't been able to solve the riddle of what kind of funny business is going on just yet, since it's only been happening for twenty years. When he does there's going to be hell to pay. But this trick has been going on since high school and holidays from college and the fifteen years after, and nothing's changed so far. It's hard to believe Old Tony has been old and blind long enough for them to pull this stunt for what seems like their entire blessed lives.

"Wait a minute," growls Old Tony. "I ain't checked it yet."

"Too late," says Miller, and keeps tapping the Big Wheel's side, making the clicking noise for Old Tony to think it's already resetting to zero.

They know Old Tony is not about to call Middle Tony up from the back, because if he did it would be like finally once and for all admitting to his son and everybody else that he can't hack it anymore. Fuck that. Old Tony wants to stay in charge around here. That damn son of his ain't done nothing to earn this place yet, even if they've all been here more than a quarter of a century. Middle Tony and Young Tony are just going to have to wait until Old Tony is in the ground to get their lunch hooks into this place.

Mick Jagger is on the radio up front telling everyone to get off his cloud while Middle Tony's voice rises above it from the back, telling his stories for tips, raunchy sagas all about Middle Tony's folk hero, The Bandit, that consistently begin with Middle Tony's favorite phrase:

"Eat shit and bark at the moon."

"The Bandit," Middle Tony informs his audience, "is gonna come up those back stairs in a little while— you gentlemen just wait and see. He'll come in here wearing a black mask and a cape and he'll be looking for some fat boys."

Middle Tony pauses for dramatic effect and takes a bite of day-old Kentucky Fried Chicken chicken livers.

Chicken livers, Middle Tony tells everybody, keep your dick hard. You boys need to be eating chicken livers every goddamn day.

"The Bandit will pick himself out one of you fat boys and put you in the barrel. Eat shit and bark at the moon. The Bandit comes out twice a week, and more if there's a full moon in the sky. The Bandit loves him some fat boys, that's for damn sure. And if he can't find any fat boys to put in the barrel, then he'll just go ahead and get him a skinny one. The skinny ones go in the pipe and the fat ones go in the barrel. Eat shit and bark at the moon."

Miller stops pecking on the side of the Big Wheel so Old Tony will think it's reset.

"It was one hundred and sixty points," David says. "That's eight dollars you owe him."

"I don't know about any eight dollars," Old Tony says.

"You do this shit every time, Tony," Miller reasons. "You act like you ain't got enough dough around here to dole out anything for a winner. You're loaded and we know it. Pay off, Tony. The man's a winner, fair and square."

Old Tony walks off grumbling to the cash register with Miller following him. When the register opens Old Tony reaches in and brings out a ten and three fives, his fingers one compartment too far to the right in the till because he is too blind to tell the difference.

Miller has a moment of Mephistopheles sitting on one shoulder and Gabriel and his trumpet sitting on the other. Old Tony is handing him twenty-five dollars instead of eight, and all he has to do is take it and no one will ever know the difference until Middle Tony's bookkeeper misses the money when it gets counted in the morning, and by then it will be too late for anybody to know what the hell has happened. Seventeen free dollars, money from heaven. Miller starts to take the bills and divide them up with everybody later or just tell everybody it was free beer provided for them by God the next couple of nights, but something in him says there is a line here that he shouldn't cross. It is one thing to win a little illegal cash from the machines, but the stash always in the end seems to go back to the Tonys and Paradise Pool. It isn't like the money ever really does go out the door and stay gone. It just circulates and keeps everyone around a little longer to spend more money. It is like Phillip always says on those infrequent times when he does happen to lose.

"Oh well, I had a lot of fun."

It takes a while to convince Old Tony he is shelling out too much money, suspicious as he is of everything, but Miller persists and comes away with the eight bucks, feeling almost like he is one righteous guy for not bilking Old Tony. Old Tony, of course, wanted to argue about it, kept right on believing Miller was trying to fleece him in some sort of reverse con job, but finally took the money back and carefully counted out the original eight dollars. He was not about to let these fellows get the best of him, no matter how many years they keep coming in here trying to get away with something.

Miller is so into this sudden abnormal spell of honesty that he hands the eight dollars over to Phillip at the Big Wheel and then ambles over to another money-sucking machine and plays until he has lost eight bucks from his own pocket. By this time Middle Tony is up from the back turning off the lights and getting ready to close. It is midnight and Christmas is over, now officially a thing of the past.

Arriving back in Dino's parking lot, the five of them huddle together like buffalo before they head home for the night. The effects of all the beer from earlier in the evening are long gone by now, everybody is mainly sober, and they form a circle between the cars to share a post-Christmas joint before heading out. The official first day of winter was four days ago, but it doesn't feel like it yet. It is in the fifties and the night winds are from the south. For a little bit Miller would put the top down on his Volkswagen, but no use in being stupid with the way the weather's been acting. For all he knows it could be raining like a son of a bitch any minute on the way home, sleeting or snowing just like that, and then he'd really be screwed up. He thinks of the two-mile drive to the store in the morning with wet seats to sit on and how much fun it would be counting money and doing the books from Christmas Eve in the office with a soggy butt. But, then, look at Sammy with that damned Corvette of his. He rides around in that thing all the time with the fiberglass top off, rain or shine or whatever and never has a second thought about it. A little precipitation has never bothered him one single bit, but of course Sammy is crazy as hell and always has been, so it's a moot point.

"So," David says, "it's Christmas night, and here we all are out playing pinball and shooting pool the same exact damn way we've been doing since we were back in high school. That's at least twenty years by my count. Sounds to me like not much has changed with us. Most people our age are home with their families now. They've got wives and kids and shit like that. Out of the five of us only one of us is still married. Phillip, you're the only one. Miller hasn't ever been married and probably never will."

"It's not my fault Cinderella hasn't showed up at the ball yet," says Miller.

"You wouldn't be at the damn ball anyway, Prince Charming," Sammy says. "You'd be off somewhere screwing the Fairy Godmother inside the pumpkin."

"Look who's talking."

"I've been married two times now," David continues. "Sammy, you're divorced, and John, you're in contention too with number one under your belt. Out of all of us, what have we got? One kid grand total? At our age that's not much of a track record.""So, what are you saying, David?" Sammy grins. "We're not normal or something? Let me call the newspaper with this big scoop."

"I've been thinking we're all disgraces to mankind for a long time now," John says. "I guess this kind of confirms it."

"I'm just saying it's pretty damn weird to me how life seems to evolve for everybody else on the face of the earth but we all just mostly stay the same," says David. "It's a mystery to me why that is."

"We're still the same," Miller sings in his Bob Seger voice. "We still aim high."

"I know what you mean, though," Phillip says. "I'm married, got a kid and all that stuff, yet here I am out with you guys. You know why? Because I can't stand to be around my wife's family is why. I was there for Christmas Eve last night and had breakfast with them this morning and then ran out the door as fast as I could, making this excuse how John needed me to help him move some furniture from his parents' house. I make up shit like this every time I come to town because I can't tolerate any part of Janet's family, can't stand to be around them too long. And it's not like it's all my fault either. Most of it's because the more I'm around them the more I'm convinced they hate me. They're a bunch of dyed in the wool Silent Majority Evangelical Christians chomping at the bit waiting for Jonathon Edwards' Angry God to hurry up and pluck me and all the rest of the sinners in the world up and throw us into the everlasting fiery pit. They've hated my guts since I made the big mistake of telling them I voted for George McGovern back in 1972."

"That was pretty stupid on your part, but it's not so much the McGovern thing," Miller says. "It's that fact that their daughter has up and married a heathen that itches their butts so much."

"That too," Phillip agrees.

"Well, I have to ask the burning question for us inquiring minds," Sammy says to John. "Did it freak you out seeing Carol at Dino's tonight? I got to admit I'm not quite over it yet. I was sitting there expecting you to cause a great big ruckus and all, and you walk up there like you're the Abington Chamber of Commerce welcoming committee and butter didn't have a chance of melting in your mouth. Hell, if it had been me I probably would have put my fist through the front window just to scare the shit out of both of them."

"I thought it might be a good idea to be cool and not get arrested on Christmas night," John smiles. "Getting locked up for the holidays has never been one of my major life ambitions."

"Do I know you?" David asks, getting up close and looking John in the face. "Has some alien come down and taken over your body? Because you're sure as hell not the John Chapman I used to know."

"I've decided to go straight in my old age," John says.

"Six more days," Sammy says, changing the subject, "and the old store is done for. I don't know about anybody else, but just that fact alone is starting to freak me out. Heck, it doesn't seem like that long ago we opened that place up. Remember opening day after the remodel? We were all there. God, I remember the damn dairy case going out that weekend and all the canned biscuits popping out all over the aisle and everybody throwing dough at each other for fifteen minutes until Mr. Overton came back there and made us stop. I thought I was going to get my ass fired right there and then."

"I've got to get by and visit the place one last time," Phillip muses, "say goodbye to the old place."

"You can come in tomorrow and grab yourself a time card and help us out if you want to," Miller says. "I'll put you on the payroll in a split second. You can pretend it's the old days and you need the money to buy yourself a car and go off to school and earn yourself another worthless degree. They'll be bulldozing the place as soon as they can next week so they can get the new store up and going, so if you're missing the place there's no time to waste. Where the building is right now will be part of the new parking lot before you can blink your goddamn eye, so better come while you can."

"I'm telling you, I'm not looking forward to any of this shit," Sammy says. "I'd about rather French kiss a brown recluse spider than clock in at that new store. It's already driving me crazy just listening to everybody talking about how wonderful everything over there is, everybody acting like nobody's supposed to even take a shit back in the goddamn bathroom or something because it's so fucking new and pretty and it's a shame to ruin it. Makes me feel like going in and messing up stuff just for the hell of it."

"Six days," Miller says, "like it or not, guys. By this time next week, it's a whole new ballgame for everybody."

MONDAY, DECEMBER 26

Miller is the first one in the door this hungover post-Christmas morning. Being at the store early and alone is nothing new or unusual, since he has his own key and lives down the street and is the earliest riser in the history of mankind, preferring never to give bad dreams an extra shot at him lingering there in the bed like there's a bullseye attached to his psyche.

He can't help being the way he is, showing up like this long before actual opening time. It is not that he loves working so much, but there is something about his being here in a private, holy place alone that seems to be good for his soul. He likes knowing that no one is going to immediately begin whining for his assistance because of some tragic circumstance the moment he walks in the door, and he likes the deliciousness of hearing whatever music might be playing at random over the intercom—it had been him who got rid of the elevator music and campaigned to get the store playing pop songs from a radio station of the past and present in the background that generally didn't make a guy want to go for the throat of the next human being he sees—and sometimes in the early darkness before dawn, in this sweet solitude, he will hear a song and know that a benevolent God of Music has added it onto the Celestial Playlist just for his ears. For years he has learned how the first fifteen minutes of being alone within the walls of Overton's Market is a provider of food and enrichment for his psychological self, and if he can only have this sort of peace for a miniscule piece of time before the rest of the world awakens he figures he can handle whatever the remainder of the day brings, which, he feels, has never been too much to ask in a world where most everybody wants everything.

He makes his way up the dog food aisle when he hears a door close with a thump from the frozen food section. If this was his first morning alone inside the Market this sound might make him jump some, could possibly cause him to wonder what was going on one aisle over causing such a commotion when he knows he is the only person present in the store at the moment, but he has walked these aisles of Overton's Market for twenty-two years now and knows every click and vibration this old building makes in the course of a day. This opening and closing of the freezer door is not the work of any employee or customer or vendor, not this early in the morning before all the lights are on and the automated doors switched on and unlocked. He has heard this type of sound and activity various and sundry times on these early mornings when it is just him inside these walls, so this audible commotion is nothing new. He remembers how at first sounds like this used to freak him out in the mornings, but that had been a long time ago, and this is now and he is used to it.

It is only Bill, he tells himself. Bill being around in the early morning is nothing to get worked up about.

The thing is Bill once worked here at Overton's, but it has been a while now since old Bill had clocked out for good and left the payroll completely and didn't require being on the weekly schedule anymore, however it was it needed to be stated, since the facts are Bill is deader than a doornail and has been for years. Bill was an old guy who'd already retired from Food Lion before he got bored sitting around and took a part-time position the first week the Market opened all those years back. He had wanted to work no more than fifteen hours a week there at first, but the grocery business was in Bill's blood, and he soon found himself adding a day here and a day there to his schedule until finally he was full-time again and coming in on his off days just to make sure everything was Jake and going along okay.

Bill liked working the bread most of all. The bread rack was his baby. He kept everything consistently neat and clean and perfectly stocked, the loaves of bread turned the right way with the wrappers gleaming in the fluorescent light like somebody had come in and taken a picture to show in a catalog of how a bakery department really needed to look, the bags of rolls, the cinnamon and raisin breads with their icy crusts, the sweet goods and doughnuts in their sections perfectly arranged and rotated on the tables in front of the racks.

Miller passes by the bread rack now and sees how empty it is, wiped out on Christmas Eve by everybody and his brother. No wonder Bill is stirring around this morning.

By six—an hour before opening time—Miller and Sammy are stocking and trying to put the store back together for Monday and the rest of this final week. Most every department is pretty much wiped out, and since starting today there aren't going to be any more deliveries it is going to be a challenge having something on the shelves for customers to buy. Bananas that are ripe this Monday morning are not going to make it the rest of the week, and what good is a grocery store without bananas? Or canned goods? Or ground beef and bread, ice cream and milk?

Not too damned good at all, Miller thinks.

The two managers and the rest of Overton's employees are already over at the new store learning to operate scanners and computer programming and how to run a cash register in the event nobody decides to show up for work. Staffing has never been a problem at old Overton's, with its five checkout lanes and tiny front office and eight compact aisles packed with groceries, meat, produce, frozen food, dairy, and the one quarter of an aisle devoted to over the counter drugs. There has never been a deli or bakery or floral shop at old Overton's, no specialty alcoves whatsoever, but there are plenty at the new store beginning with next week's opening. The only problem is finding enough people to fill all the positions there. Abington is not the largest town on the map. Its population is not exactly burgeoning.

The old Overton's is almost a thing of the past now, and Miller is the guy left in charge of the shell. Sammy is around, handling the grocery department and dairy and frozen food all by his lonesome, and this morning Phillip is coming in to put in some hours helping out. The two of them left behind here have to do a whole lot of everything on this duo skeleton crew, check, bag, stock what's left to go out, clean up messes, but it's not as bad as it sounds. After Christmas business always drops off anyway—nobody has any money left from splurging on the holiday—and there's not going to be too much left here at old Overton's for anyone to buy either on this Monday or for the rest of the week anyway, so it's really just a matter of both of them showing up and going through the motions.

By noon the word seems to be out that Overton's really is going out of business for sure, that they haven't been kidding all these weeks when the big building behind the store started going up, and how there isn't much of a point in going in and shopping because there is not much of anything left to buy.

Might as well go across town to Food Lion or Kroger, people think, that seems to be the obvious solution, but a lot of the old faithful customers can't help but find themselves drawn through the doors anyway. Like vultures, they sniff around and sense something dead. They come inside one more time to see if there's anything in the old store for them to nibble on and scavenge.

Later on, there's a lot of standing around on the front walk. Miller and Phillip fire up Marlboros and Sammy runs a rag across the hood of his Vette and wonders if he ought to pull a joint from his pocket so the three of them can stand out here good and high and watch the traffic going by on Clement Road. They could get a good buzz while they're getting paid, which would almost make presiding over this end of the world scene they've got going here a hell of a lot more tolerable than watching it happen in their right minds.

"We better not," Miller says. "It would be about my luck somebody will find out and we'll get our asses fired and then have to miss out on getting to work in the magical store of the future next week. I don't know if I could stand the disappointment. My life would be in shambles."

"Besides," Phillip says, "we might actually have a real live customer come in at some point to shop, and then here we'd all three be, too ripped to check them out and take their money."

"We could always just give everything away," Sammy says.

"Great idea," says Phillip. "That way we could eliminate having to haul what's left over to the new store."

"Piss on that," Sammy says. "If there's anything left Saturday it can go home with me. I'm thinking about borrowing John's truck and loading up."

"You can probably," Miller tells him, "get what's left in the front seat of the Vette."This is the way this last Monday goes, slow, sad, a day kin to a dirge. Now and then they go inside and straighten displays, throw away trash; all too soon there is no work for them to do and they end up outside on the walk again, viewing the empty lot with no cars in it and watching the sun go down. They plan the approaching night, where to eat, what to drink. They call David at work and John at his parents' house and plan to gather somewhere later.

It's the holidays and everyone is at least all present and accounted for in the same town at the same time. It's almost like it used to be, minus old Overton's closing down, of course, but almost. There's still lots to talk about, maybe not so much as there used to be, no new women or weird romantic entanglements or movies or exotic drugs that take you to new strange places, but there is still enough to pass the time. They can talk about the time the store got stuck up on a summer night when they were all there to see it—two guys with handkerchiefs over their noses like they were in an old timey western or something, waving handguns around that turned out to be BB pistols. They can talk about their high lottery numbers back during the Viet Nam days, how everybody got lucky and nobody had to go get shot at. They can talk about the night Martin Luther King got killed and how the store closed early for curfew, how they stood on the sidewalk and listened to gunshots going off over in the projects ten miles away and wondering if the angry blacks from that side of town were going to venture over their way looking for somebody to shoot or something to burn, how they were frightened of what was happening in the world but didn't want to talk about it, but chose rather to talk about girls and getting drunk and who was screwing who at the moment. Miller and Sammy can even get a laugh recalling how they once spent two weeks torturing a car salesman at a used car lot up Clement drive, calling him night and day asking about a yellow Volkswagen parked at the front of the lot, a convertible with a sign on it that said *Sun Bug! Runs Good!* Walter was the guy's name, Miller laughed, do you remember Walter, and Sammy said yeah. How they would go by and let Walter show them the car, open the trunk and look at the engine, slam the doors, put the top up and down, turn the radio off and on. Haggle over the price. Miller keeping Walter going, playing him for a fool, and then the next thing he knew he found himself actually liking the car, looking it over for real and then finally buying it. And telling Walter how he and Sammy thought old Walter had earned every cent of his commission. That was fifteen years ago and Miller still has his yellow Sun Bug. Best car I ever had, he tells everybody.

There's one week to go and here they all are one more time. And the store's not gone yet, not totally, and neither are they. Things will be different next week and next year but that's all a long way off for the moment. Everything goes away eventually, hell, they know that, but not this coming night, not this week, not this moment.

There's still now. Now is not the long ago just yet.

TUESDAY, DECEMBER 27

Phillip pours himself a second cup of coffee and sits in the den enjoying the silence of his in-law's house. His five-year-old, Melanie, has spent the night sleeping with her grandparents, or the Holy Sticklers, as Phillip likes to think of them, while he has slept with Janet in Janet's old bedroom, lying in bed and thinking of Janet as a younger version of herself and how he spent a lot of time back in the faraway past trying to figure out how to get her and him in this location at the same time for something other than conversation. That was more than twenty years ago. He hates to come right out and admit such heresy, but he likes not having his daughter underfoot, and he supposes such an attitude can only mean he is a genuinely piss-poor father. Probably true, he knows, but there are other factors. He teaches at a small college, and during his classes he hears young men and women emitting sounds that don't matter so much whatsoever in the great realm of things all the time, so that when he does have the luxury of getting away by himself the lack of human amplitude is like a gift from heaven, or at least a small, healing salve that keeps his brain from rupturing and oozing out all over the place like the Blob in the old Steve McQueen movie. He does his best, though, to keep such anti-social feelings as these to himself, but he can tell Janet knows his mental slant and most of the time tries to make it where her husband of fifteen years doesn't crash on the rocks from his maladies and come up missing and leave her a widow and his daughter an orphan.

For a while he sits in the quiet of the room with a cat named Scratchy in his lap, but after a few more minutes of peace he decides to go over to John's parents' house and pick John up for an early lunch. When he and John are both back in Abington they have a tradition of going to Chan's Chinese Cottage for a dose of Chinese food, to wolf down bowls of Wonton soup and entrees and slurp hot tea. Chan's is not the greatest Chinese restaurant in the world--there are several newer places that have opened in Abington in the past few years that are much better--but Chan's has been around forever, and that counts for something. Phillip and John used to go pig out at Chan's back in high school, would meet there after baseball or track meets or school games or work at Overton's to fill their bellies, and it is hard to change now. If they went and ate at another restaurant they wouldn't be able to order the same thing, and what would that say for old times and Auld Lang Syne?

The house John grew up in hasn't changed all that much, but maybe Phillip, being a creature who has always rebelled against change, doesn't notice the new additions as much as someone else does. He guesses if he were to really study the place there would be a few differences—a new roof, a chain link fence installed sometime in the last decade, shutters painted a dark green now instead of the brown shade they'd been for so long. The old stand-alone garage is gone, torn down and replaced with some tin structure where a family of Munchkins could easily exist. The biggest thing Phillip truly does notice missing—and he can never get accustomed to it being absent—is the old basketball backboard and rim that hung from the front of the extinct garage. Sometime or another it was relegated to the dump along with the rotting woods of the old garage, a number of years after John was long-gone in his adult life and none of the boys were around anymore to dribble on the pavement and shoot basketball until dark. The new Munchkin abode is rimless and backboardless; nobody has to measure off where the foul line is. It seems pretty strange to Phillip for something that was so important in their glorious boyhood past to not be around anymore. So much, he thinks, for holy shrines.

It is always a little strange coming back to Abington, even if he isn't ever separated from it for all that terribly long of a time. It is still always like an abrupt jump into the canyons of the past.

John and his parents are in the kitchenette drinking coffee when Phillip taps on the storm door at the side of the house, sitting there together with mugs in the tiny yellow alcove surrounded by familiar pictures of woodsy cabins on the walls and a black cat clock with a tail swishing back and forth marking the passing seconds. Mr. Chapman is retiring this year after thirty years with Abington Electric and Mrs. Chapman is still holding down her position as school secretary for Tidwell Elementary, so they're enjoying this extra day off together. Becky, John's sister, would be right here with the three, Phillip thinks, just like it had always been when he'd come over here as a kid and a teenager, but Becky was dead of breast cancer six years ago. John hasn't mentioned Becky biting the dust in a while, but that is fairly normal, since John has since the beginning of time gone long spells without mentioning much of anything going on in his life or anybody else's, being either secretive as hell or not wanting to know about anything happening outside of his own backyard and at the same time certainly not wanting to air soap opera chapters of his own daily story for public airing.

John has been a goddamn clam for years.

"Sit down and have a cup of coffee," Mrs. Chapman says. "We're just sitting here shooting the breeze catching up. We're working on our third pot already."

"None for me, thanks," Phillip smiles. "I've had my two cups this morning. Any more caffeine than that and I get strung out and start bouncing off walls."

"If you'd break out that bottle of Jim Beam up there in the cabinet, Dad," John states, "I'll bet good money Phillip can put a little dent in that for you. He's a whole lot fonder of alcohol than he is coffee."

"Yeah, I bet he could. I remember when you two were boys sneaking around and doing just that very thing, secretly lowering the contents of my bottles of whiskey," Mr. Chapman says, "back when you thought I didn't have sense enough to notice how it was slowly disappearing on me. Take you a few sips and then water it down so I wouldn't notice anything was missing. But I knew all right."

"How come you never said anything about it?" Phillip asks.

"Because I was waiting to catch you two in the act, that's why, and then I was going to make you both wish you'd never been born. I had plans to make you fellows do all sorts of work around here so John could keep his car and so I wouldn't be tempted to call your daddy up and tell him what my only son and you had recently been up to. But you boys were both pretty crafty, pretty doggone sneaky, I'll give you credit for that. I never could catch you red-handed."

Snowflake the poodle walks in and wags her tail weakly at Phillip. He bends down and scratches the top of her head.

"God, Snowflake," he says. "You're still here. You're as old as I am."

"She's one hundred and twenty-six in dog years," John says. "She's eternal. She's about like Boris Karloff was in 'The Mummy.' She was around when we built the pyramids."

"We didn't build the pyramids," Phillip reminds him.

"We didn't?" John says. "Are you sure of that? Because I feel like I did sometimes. I feel like, with a little bit of effort, I could be older than a big ancient pile of Egyptian dirt."

***

One of their favorite things to do when going to eat at Chan's is to get high on the way over. That's not the case today, since John and Phillip don't happen to possess any pot between them. This is a personal decision on both their parts, one that mostly stems from the fact that John and Phillip both have decent jobs at the moment and are not chomping at the bit to do anything to screw up a good thing. All John would have to do in a Hooterville kind of town like McGinnis is get caught even standing somewhere near a nickel bag or a joint and that would be curtains for him as far as employment goes. And even though John is pretty sure that half the technicians and linemen and meter readers at McGinnis Electric are either heads or drunks or both, it is still the type of place where a guy needs to keep his personal life nice and distant from the watchful eye of headquarters. John does not really want to think about perhaps having someone constantly keeping an eye on him and having to function day to day at his job under a lingering cloud of suspicion. There are even rumors that drug testing may be on the way in the future at McGinnis Electric, so he makes it a point to stay as clean as possible. The pay is good, and he doesn't want to do anything to stop the money he's making from rolling in. He's already lost one house to a divorce; it's going to take some time and accrued money before he can get around to buying another. No sense in delaying things further just for the sake of grooving to a song and maybe getting ripped enough to perhaps catch a momentary glimpse of God.

It's still a little early for lunch, so they decide to take a mystery tour, a traditional excursion they like indulging in when they are back in the old hometown at the same time. John wheels his truck past their old elementary school, then cruises by the middle school just around the corner, putters past churches and locations where movie houses used to stand but are no more, replaced now with furniture stores and mattress warehouses, and then heads on past their old high school that looks nothing like it did twenty years back, renovated as it is now, added on and torn down several times, and currently painted a different color.

Amid the sight-seeing it becomes time to play the game of how it was and how it is, who was here and where did these folks all end up. This is a game that always occurs on the mystery tour. It starts out so familiar most of the time and then has surprises hiding down every street, in the yard of every murky house, haunted memories and images of a distant but still very nearby past.

They pass by a convenience market that was a Handy Pantry in their time. Bars adorn the windows and doors to keep thieves from breaking in during the nights. Beer signs are illuminated, money orders are sold inside. If a pack of cigarettes or a twelve-pack is your craving, this must be the place.

"Remember buying baseball cards here?" John asks. "Sitting on the curb opening them up and cramming all that sweet gum in your mouth?"

"They had a bin over in the corner that sold 45 records for next to nothing. I thought I was getting a real deal until I got home and discovered nothing was by the original artists. What I thought was a Beach Boys record was actually getting sung by the Beach Brothers or the Beach Baptists or something like that. I didn't read for detail too good back then."

"Bet you don't remember the name of the store manager? Always said, 'What else, son?'"

"Ed Autry. I called him Mister Gene. That's because I was then and still am now so fucking clever."

Down Emerson Drive they see a row of houses where a field of thickets used to be. The weeds and vegetation are chopped down and cheap, tiny houses stand in rows, eight in a consecutive line like uniformed soldiers all looking no different from the other.

"We smoked our first cigarette there," Phillip points out. "What were we—ten?"

"Twelve, I think," John says. "It was a Raleigh filter. I don't remember where I got it."

"Save the coupons, get an iron lung."

After a few more twists and turns John drives by a road with a private entrance and a sign that says there's to be no trespassing. He wonders what is back down that road these days, if it's like a nudist colony or a place to worship the devil and sacrifice a few goats, but he doesn't turn in. It's not like he really wants to know.

"I got caught by the cops parking down there with Linda Cole one night. Remember me telling you about it? I had to hustle like hell to get my pants on when I saw the police car coming. Spoiled the whole night and scared the shit out of me too. I never came close to getting my hands on old Linda again. She thought she got saved from me by an act of God or something."

"She was probably right. You've been an ambassador from Hell for a while now."

They pull in at Chan's. There is only one other car in the lot, and since it is now officially lunchtime this is not to be construed as a good sign. Such a lack of business might indicate an inferior product being offered, but Phillip and John don't really derive any caution from such an omen. They both know nothing has changed here all that much, seeing that Chan's has been fairly poor and persistently paltry and consistently inferior from the beginning and has managed to stay that way for years, and if it had ever changed too much they would not have recognized it and not had affection for it as the same old place.

They are seated at a table by a pretty Chinese girl who is probably a great-granddaughter of Mr. Chan and who they both know from past experience they will never see again. This is standard Chan procedure through the years. You enter the door and are met with some ethereal, fragile beauty who sends your sensibilities fluttering out to far, poetic places, you sit in the darkness and view a menu promising good health and exalted taste, and then Chan's wrinkled wife or oldest unmarried daughter shows up and you order what you're looking at on the menu while trying not to look at warts and liver spots or think about the possibility that what you are about to eat may be one of the neighborhood cats that have gone missing in the past day or two.

"A Pu Pu Platter for me," John says. He looks up at the server and fixes her with a grin. "It says for two, but it's all for me. I've got a big appetite. I'm what you folks call a capitalistic pig."

The woman does not smile, but simply scribbles on a green pad.

"You?" she says to Phillip.

"Sizzling Wor Ba and Won Ton soup." She gathers the menus as if they are something valuable and disappears behind a dark curtain, where it is possible someone is adding a cat to a kettle this very moment. Cat references have always been in the conversation at Chan's, and it would not seem like a traditional outing here without the subject coming up.

"You're not working with Miller and Sammy today?" John asks. "I thought Miller said there was so much to get done this week and no time to do it."

"There's nothing much left to sell there but absolute crap and there's nothing coming in to stock either. I don't know why the damn Overtons are going through the motions of even staying open this week, because the place is getting empty as hell and almost nobody's coming in to shop. Of course you do have the usual goobers dropping in to see if anything's being given away yet, the cash registers, the check lanes, the fixtures. I keep expecting them to go back to the restrooms and try and pull out the commodes before it's all over with. It's kind of sad really."

"You're right. It's too bad. The Market was a good store for a long time. I worked there off and on ten years, and I always liked it. I never minded coming to work too much because I always had a good time when I got there. All you guys were usually there working and it was like a party I got paid to go to."

"Yeah, we all pretty much grew up in that store. And now they're reducing it to rubble right in front of our eyes. It's not pretty. I'm kind of like Miller. I'm starting to take it personally."

The food arrives and they eat silently, surprised at how hungry they are and how Chan's food tastes good to them even when they ought to know better. Phillip keeps glancing across the room at two women in a booth that is obscured by the lack of illumination Chan's has always favored, a trick, it is said, to keep the customer from recognizing the Siamese cat from down the street that has just been brought in on a platter, and thinking how he knows this feline from somewhere but can't think of where it was and doesn't really want to remember. Faces and voices he cannot immediately place, he believes, are better off staying forgotten, since bad memories are generally the first things the mind relishes repressing, but he goes ahead and points the two out to John anyway.

"Tell me if you recognize those women?"

"I think one of them used to be Vickie Carlisle, buddy, but I wouldn't swear to it. If it is, then the years haven't been very kind to her. I don't know, though. I'd have to get closer to see. The truth be told all I ever really looked at was old Vickie's ass, so I don't know if I can make a positive identification with her sitting down like that."

Phillip strains his eyes and looks closer.

"Is that her mother with her? Or is who we think is Vickie actually her mother and the other woman her grandmother? Because, god, John, look at them. They're fossils. How can any female we both wanted to jump in bed with grow up looking like this?"

"She doesn't look that bad to me," John says. "You're just picky. You always have been."

"I've just got this aversion to death," Phillip says, picking up a solitary shrimp and taking a bite. "That's what these two look like to me. Death warmed over."

"Well now, a little necrophilia never hurt anybody."

The sun is shining when they leave, but a cold west wind is blowing and Phillip is glad to get inside the truck. They drive down Clement Avenue and it is almost deserted, people home for the holidays, off work and out of school. Phillip thinks how at this time next week he will be preparing to go back to teaching, getting his lectures ready, preparing his mind to deal with students again, to snap them and himself back into a routine after a long Christmas break. He remembers how Christmas break always was for him growing up—he wanted to disappear inside it and never return. Coming back was always a drag.

John drives along looking at the stretch of Clement and noticing how small it seems to him. He punches in the lighter and sticks a cigarette in his mouth. He thinks of Vickie Carlisle and agrees with Phillip. God, she was old. How could she look like that so soon? He thinks of watching her walk down the hallway at school all those years back, how he'd study her without even giving her a name. She was faceless then, she is faceless now. He realizes how it is starting to get like that a lot every day now. Strange, he thinks. Strange the way I'm getting and strange the way I remember I was. I'm not too impressed with myself, either then or now. Sometimes there's a lot of change, sometimes there isn't, and it doesn't seem to matter to me one way or the other. Sometimes I feel like I'm getting creepier every day just on my own and I don't know how to stop it.

"Anything you want to do?" he asks. "I can't really think of anything too exciting."

"Let's go by the store," Phillip says. "It's just Sammy and Miller there. We can sit around and shoot the shit a while."

"That sounds original."

"You know me. Always full of good ideas."

***

Surprisingly, a few cars are actually in the lot when they get to the market, and when they go inside Miller has several customers in his line. Sammy stands behind him sacking an order that is piled high on the check stand along with what has already been bagged and in the bascart.

"Everything's one-third off," Sammy explains.

"One-third off a bunch of crap is still crap," John mutters. "What's in here that anybody could possibly want to buy?"

"Wait until they get to half off," Phillip says. "All this stuff will go like hotcakes."

Miller, as he's been telling everyone for years, is the fastest checker who's ever lived. He is greased lightning when it comes to punching in numbers. He is faster than a speeding bullet scanning items. He has memorized every code for everything, produce, ice, postage stamps, you name it. He knows every shortcut, how to get around every obstacle that might slow him down. They don't call me Flash for nothing, he tells everybody all the time, has told them this since back before Jonah got swallowed by the whale.

Nobody's ever called you Flash anytime, they always tell him back.

Miller, though, is damn fast and everybody knows it. It only takes him around three minutes to weed out the long line of people, get the three huge orders checked out and bagged and paid and out the door. For a minute Phillip is tempted to go jump in his old lane, good old Number Five down at the end, but he can see how by the time he got there it would be too late—Miller would have already gotten rid of the traffic. In the old days, when they were in high school and working all the hours they could, all five of them would man the registers on Saturdays and see who could check out the most people, ring up the most sales, take in the most money. Back then there were only a few ways to pay, cash or check, maybe paper food stamps, perhaps a credit card every blue moon or so, but that was unusual and annoying as hell. You had to stop and get a plastic machine out of the office equipped with carbon paper and perforations and you had to line the paper up with the indentions of the card and the order total written in. It took you about five minutes to jump through every hoop and climb every mountain just to get the transaction over with, and by the time you finished you were so far behind everybody else you were racing against checking you knew you'd never be able to catch up. And it would piss you off because the four losers had to buy the winner food and beer later on that night, and goddamn it, they all remember how most of the time it was damn

Miller who won. Miller was the fastest and they could have called him Flash.

But they didn't. Fuck that. He would have loved hearing them say it too much.

It's going to be like this the rest of the week. Every day the prices are going to go down a little more. Jim Overton and his sister Deanna Overton-McFarland came by this morning and told Miller and Sammy the strategy. Data processing programs would get run each night to automatically reflect each day's discount, and flip charts would be printed up to tell them what to charge on labeled goods. This came from the owners, so Miller and Sammy shook their heads and said yes, but in their minds they knew they'd do what they wanted to do and what needed to be done until the last day of business came. It wasn't like there was going to be anybody around to tell them any different, like somebody was going to actually be present over here to see what was going on. It wasn't like anybody already over at the new store gave a shit or would ever know any different, and it wasn't like anybody had tried to tell either one of them what to do for a long time now either, and it figures nobody is going to start telling them now. Mostly, Miller and Sammy have been left alone to do what they wanted, what they thought best, and that was the way they liked it.

Truly, it wasn't like anybody really gave a shit what they did. That was the way it has been at the Market for a long time now. There is the rest of the store, and then there is them, Miller and Sammy. For a good while there was also Phillip and David and John, and it was like the five of them were always there together working as a team, doing their thing and pulling the store through whatever storm arose, and everybody else just backed off and let them do it.

It had always worked out, so what was the point in changing anything now?

***

If there is one good thing about closing down the Market, it means nobody has to work nights anymore. Since the store is closing at five during this last week the doors can be locked and everyone can be out in plenty of time to grab something to eat and see what else is happening around Abington. With John and Phillip in for the holidays, this gives the five of them more time to hang around together like they used to back in medieval days when a brontosaurus or two could regularly be seen walking around the city limits.

Tonight, the plan is to take in a basketball game fifty miles up the interstate in Clarksville. It's only about an hour away but they need to pile in David's van and get there in time to find a place to eat before the game, so Sammy and John and Phillip drive over to Abington Home and Hardware and wait for David to get off, for since the beginning of time David has always been the driver for any of their jaunts or expeditions. Before he leaves the store, Phillip calls and tells Janet where he's going and how he'll be home as soon as they get back. She is not too happy about him spending yet another night with his friends and not being around for the evening, but he hasn't been too damn overjoyed either about once again spending his Christmas break in the company of her parents, so there's that. He hates to get snippy about her family and visiting them and having to stay under their roof for a stretch of time that feels like more of a prison sentence than hardcore criminals seem to get slapped with, but she can't expect him to stick around the place all day and night getting looked at and examined like it's his fault the world has gone to shit

50

the way that it has. And so, if he goes to a game with his old pals it doesn't mean he's making plans to abandon his wife and child or anything like that. It's just a good way of coping and staying halfway sane. Janet doesn't understand what it is to get driven around the bend. She thinks these sort of moments spent are joyous.

Miller isn't going. He doesn't tell anyone why, but just informs them he's got something else to do and doesn't want to talk about it, and gets in the Sun Bug and leaves. It's not like he's fooling anybody being tight-lipped and providing no excuse for not going along with them, because everybody's been around him for a long time and they all know pretty much in advance what old Miller does and where he goes when situations like this occur.

Everybody knows it's Laurel again. Anytime something secret and mysterious like this comes up and Miller starts acting weird, it's always damn Laurel who's at the bottom of it.

Miller opens the Sun Bug up to its absolute German best for a few seconds winding up Wright Avenue, putting the store and the guys behind him before one of them has time to ask him any stupid questions. Not that anyone is really going to say anything, since it's been a long time since anybody has ever dared say a word about Miller and the way his plans seem to change so abruptly from time to time, because that's one bridge everybody knows better than to cross. It's not as if his buddies are dumber than rocks. They know what he's up to and how it's not really going to change or ever be any of their business. He makes a wide swoop before coming in the back way of the lot to pull up behind the new store, parking in the back where the Sun Bug isn't visible from the street, because a yellow Volkswagen is going to stand out like a beacon no matter where it is. He doesn't really want Sammy and Phillip and John standing over at the old store fifty yards away seeing the Sun Bug parked beside Laurel's Acura at the new store three minutes after he's just left them going the other way. He can imagine the grinning and laughing that would go on when that went down. See? I told you, they'd say. That didn't take long, now did it? I knew where the son of a bitch was headed all the time.

Miller feels like he's been doing this kind of shit for years, which is true, the only difference is now he finds himself doing it in a different place. All the times before he has carried on with Laurel Adams-Overton under the auspices of the old store, in his apartment or house or somewhere clandestine, getting away with all this cloak and dagger stuff for he doesn't know how long, and now it's out with the old and in with the new and the setting is changing but the plot seems to be remaining the same. It's appropriate that this is the last week of the year and the old store is getting ready to meet the wrecking ball. Things have been the same and going on so long and never changing that maybe it is a good thing that the rot and decay of the old store and the new competition in town from the modern supermarkets have made it necessary for Overton's Market to rise to another level, and maybe it's good that Miller Hill has done a lot of thinking and observing while the new building has been going up and has about halfway decided within himself that he is not going to be acquiring any kind of sight in the near future that will envision him actually working in this new store and being a part of it while at the same time continuing an affair with the wife of the guy who owns it, an affair with a woman he maybe has loved in the past and maybe loves in a strange way now but who perhaps is another one of those contrivances

Miller Hill always seems to saddle himself with to feel some sort of connection with life and this world he finds himself in some way a member of, and maybe, he has decided, he is not in love at all and never has been either, and maybe it is time to get out of the forest and to some place where the trees aren't so goddamned thick that he can't see shit and he can make his mind up about a few assorted serious life-type things one damn way or the other.

He sits and waits for Laurel to come out to her car. She is getting off at five-thirty, and he will not even speak to her when she comes outside, but will just start his car and go home, knowing she is not working over and will soon be on the way. He would call her at the store, but that borders on dangerous. And stupid— don't forget stupid. She's in the front office surrounded by lots of people, including his boss and her husband Jim, who is in his own affair with some woman over at the bank he thinks nobody knows about, but who still keeps his eye on Laurel, keeping tabs on her whereabouts when he can and wondering just exactly what she's doing while he's doing the very thing he's worried about her doing. Twelve years Miller has been fooling with Laurel—two or three years before and then eight after she married Jim. Miller thinks how it was that he was thinking of marrying his old girlfriend Patricia from college back when all this rigmarole started going on, back in the Dark Ages after graduation, but decided how, no, maybe it wouldn't be the wisest thing in the world to marry somebody he was only about half-interested in when there was this Laurel woman hiring on at the store with her long legs and hair down her back and her cheekbones way up there who maybe he could be in love with someday if everything fell just right and maybe not too, but how he would sincerely hate the hell out of himself later on if he didn't go ahead and jump right in there and give the whole deal the old college try and find out.

And it is twelve years later now, but then, who's counting? And here he sits in a parking lot still giving this the old college try, and it's two days past Christmas and the Market he's grown up in is closing down and he's starting to feel a little long in the tooth trying to be some guy giving everything he's got to things that either sink or swim whether he's in the pool or not, and there's something about it all grouped together that's making him feel like something's going to have to give pretty soon or he's not going to be responsible for what goes up or what comes down.

In five minutes Laurel walks out to her car and Miller fires up the Sun Bug and heads home. His house is not far away from the store; there have been a few instances when he has actually walked the half-mile to work, but he doesn't do it on a regular basis, and he doesn't do it for fun. Once, he had a dead battery and had awakened late from a vodka hangover and had to get to work frigging pronto to open the doors, and there have been a few times when it's snowed and he'd decided to truck it on foot rather than have some dipshit slip and slide into him and total his beloved Sun Bug out. If the truth was told he doesn't really trust himself driving in the snow that much. He might possibly do something dumb and wreck the Sun Bug himself, be an idiot and drive off in a ditch. The thing of it is this is the South—nobody knows how to drive in the snow here. Hell, most folks have never even seen snow but once or twice in their entire lives, so it's hard to be an expert. Best, he believes, to stay off the target range and not take the chance.

He swings the Sun Bug off to the right when he gets to the back of the driveway so Laurel can pull into the garage and he can shut the door behind her and no one can see her car. It is like this is an exact science the way they've been doing this for so long. By the time she's pulled into the garage he's pulling down the door and she's inside the den door and he comes inside. It takes maybe five minutes for them to get undressed and to hop in between the sheets and be all over each other like they are pressed for time and there's none of it to waste.

Because they are and there isn't.

All this is going on and Miller is wondering how many times it has been precisely this way, exactly like this. There is no conversation much—that is always saved until later—and so they go about this business like it is an extension of the job they took on when they come to work in the mornings. It was a while coming when they first met, when Laurel came to work for Overton's from some chain store in Little Rock, fresh off what she called a bad marriage wanting to make a clean sweep of it in another state. She had followed her sister to Tennessee and been referred to Overton's by her brother-in-law, who happened to be a fraternity brother of Jim Overton at Ole Miss, and she was there learning to do books for the Market, and then, after a time, being courted by Jim, then the assistant manager of the place, his father Mr. Overton still working, and all the time there was Miller, in his mid-twenties, out of school and still employed there at Overton's, working there for so long he'd decided he had nowhere else to go, equipped as he was with his worthless English major that denoted him as capable of teaching and pretty much nothing else. Miller had looked Laurel up and down for a time then that first instance and believed her legs to be among the longest he'd seen, and when they began to talk they discovered they liked a lot of the same things like movies and music and books and the joint suspicion occurred to them both that it just might be they could come to like each other. This went on a few years, this workplace sort of foreplay, even while Jim's courtship of Laurel proceeded in earnest. And then came the moment when Miller and Laurel were alone in the backroom, a chance encounter on a drab rainy Wednesday, and suddenly as if scripted they had kissed by the time clock like it was something that was supposed to happen, and the only unanswered question was why did it take so long to occur and when were they going to do it again and again?

And it was right about this time when Miller Hill started wondering if the possibility existed that he might indeed be capable of falling in love. And falling in love with someone who was fixing to marry somebody else. He doubted such a scenario, but there were times when he began to have second thoughts. He thought about the way he was and how screwed up the situation was and how it seemed like such a thing was right down his alley. He thought so much about it that it seemed the correct and safe thing to do was to do nothing, to not jump into any sort of romantic fray that could get entangled and complicated and might even result in him getting fired, for then he would have no recourse but to have to go and find a teaching job, take a few more classes to get certified, and he was just too damned busy with his real life for that. Also terrified at the thought of facing something so frighteningly real to life as that. Then came the time when Laurel got tired of waiting and said yes and went ahead and married Jim Overton, and that didn't help to clear things up in his head much either.

"I was wondering if you were going to be outside tonight," Laurel says. They are finished, lying on their backs looking at the ceiling fan rotate. "I haven't heard a word from you since Christmas Eve morning. That's three days, buddy. I didn't quite know what to think."

"What with everything going on at the store and helping Santa get the reindeer hitched up I've been a trifle swamped. I knew you'd be busy family-wise on Christmas day, so I just took it easy all day and then went and shot pool Christmas night. Phillip's in visiting with his in-laws this week, so he's coming by the store helping out me and Sammy here and there some, but it's not like any of us have got time to walk over and hobnob. Believe it or not, there's still a lot to do before we shut the doors."

"You and Sammy both have to come in some time and get your training on the registers and the computers. We do have grand opening next week, just in case you've forgotten."

"I'm trying to," he says. "I'm doing the best I can to forget everything about it."

He gets out of bed and selects a mystery cigarette from a wooden box by the table. They are mystery cigarettes because Miller buys varieties of cigarettes all the time and gets free sample packs from sales reps and randomly throws them loose into the box. For some ignorant reason he likes not knowing what he is lighting up when he gets out of bed, sweet mystery of life, the song starts up in his head every time he reaches in the box. This would drive a lesser person crazy, but he is just nuts enough to like it. "Jim says the inventory is getting pretty low over there," Laurel says, "and there may not be enough stock left to warrant even staying open through Saturday."

"Jim doesn't know but what I tell him. He hasn't been by but once or twice in the last two weeks to see what's going on. He just calls and spouts off what he thinks we ought to do each day."

Miller is not so thrilled about engaging in a conversation about Laurel's darling husband right now, so he dresses and walks out to the kitchen to see if, after Laurel leaves, he has something here to eat or if he's going to have to go out and get something. There's leftover chicken, but from when? He can't remember when he made it, if it is pre-Christmas vintage or what. It might, however, be fairly tasty if he really wants to put an end to it all. Fall dead from botulism on the kitchen floor and the new Overton's would have to open without him. Perhaps a small tragedy, but the show must go on. That's entertainment.

"You and me aren't doing so good right now, are we?"

Laurel stands in the doorway, arms folded, dressed, ready, it looks, to either go or stay. He looks at her and understands why he might be in love with her—she's great, she's pretty, she has a wonderful smile—but he thinks of her Acura out in the garage and how it's sitting there with the sliding door down and how in a few minutes their time will be done and he'll have to go out and open the door and watch her drive away. He thinks of how then the only thing that will matter much the rest of the night is if he has to order a pizza or not.

Happy frigging holidays.

He thinks how this kind of shit is not really what he had in mind the first time he saw her. He thinks he was looking for something else, but he's damned if he's been able to put his finger on exactly what that was just yet.

***

As a duo, John and Phillip have had a good time messing with David since elementary school, teaming up and doing their best to drive him nuts whenever possible, so after all these years it's not like they are fixing to stop now. When it's time to climb into David's van to make the trip to Clarksville, they allow Sammy to grab the front shotgun seat, then they scurry back like demonic children to the furthest rear seats to park themselves by the back window. They sit grinning at each other watching David search the rearview mirror in an attempt to see what they are up to back there. They see his eyes darting around in the reflection, and they know they are successfully driving him crazy the way they've always aspired to do.

"I know what you're up to, so don't even start," David says. "You guys ought to try growing up one of these days. See what life as an adult is like. You might even like it."

It is very seldom that David drinks, like almost never, and he has never joined in with everyone else in smoking pot or partaking of any recreational drugs, so this abstinence has over the years earned him the status of designated driver before designated drivers were a cool thing to have around. It had never taken much urging to get David to fulfill this position for the most part, since he has always, besides being a habitual tee-totaler, been a complete and total control freak, so driving his van and holding the power to stop and go and turn right or left on his own has always meant a great deal to him. Because of this psychological dependency the other four guys have been able to sit back and leave the driving to David and enjoy the luxury of getting out of their respective trees with no dire consequences or responsibilities to ever have to fret about.

But there is something about David that simply begs for a little more than merely being his passengers, and very early on John and Phillip latched on to another one of their long-standing traditions.

David has always loved vans. His family had owned vans since he was a child, and a van was what he had first learned to drive on. Vans had room for boom boxes and tape players and ice chests and anything else a guy might want to carry along and not leave at home. Jackets, blankets, lawn chairs, you name it—you could always be prepared for anything if you owned a van. So David bought a used Chevy van for his first car and has owned some kind of van since.

It was in summer after high school graduation when Phillip and John saw a city van pull up beside them at a red light. Peering out the window of the vehicle were the faces of several handicapped people, blank unfathoming eyes staring into space at something unseen or fixed, peering at John and Phillip and the contours of David's own van with intense fascination like it was all, like everything else in the world, a source of wonder, lost rapture frozen on their faces, eyes wide and jaws agape and heads tilted. The faces looked at John and Phillip intently, studying their mysterious countenances for all they were worth, and John and Phillip looked back.

Without a word being exchanged between them Phillip and John then moved from their seats behind David at the wheel to the back of the van. Looking out the window they transformed their own personas into images of their personal versions of these recently-observed less fortunate, fixed their faces and eyes and jaws to look afflicted and blank and lost in some detached reality while adding some drooling on the window to make their visages appear all the more authentic to anyone in traffic who might cast their eyes upon them.

"What are you guys doing back there?" David had asked.

"Just riding along in our handicapped van," John said. "Why have a cool van like this if you don't have a couple of afflicted folks to ride in it?"

David told them to stop, cursed them and threatened to never let them ride in his van again, told them how they should be ashamed of themselves for making fun of people who couldn't help being the way they were, and Phillip and John agreed, told him back how they couldn't help being the way they were too, and thank you, David, for driving us to places we couldn't possibly get to by ourselves. You're our hero, they told him.

Twenty years this had been going on. At least twenty years, maybe more. John and Phillip can never seem to get enough of it. Sammy always smiles when it starts. David curses.

"Jesus," David says. "You fuckers never quit, do you?"

"Not in this lifetime," says John.

They ride through traffic with John and Phillip pressing their contorted astonished faces to the glass and waving at people and grinning like they'd had their day made when people wave back. Finally, they hit the interstate and speed toward Clarksville, listening to

David's same old Moody Blues cassette play, the cassette he never changes from the player. They ride the seesaw and aspire to be a singer in a rock and roll band all the way to a Burger King, where Whoppers hurriedly get swallowed before they find a lot to park in and go inside the gym for the game.

It is like the two teams in the building decided to have a game on this night but forgot to tell anyone about it. The gym is almost empty, big blocks of chairs and sections with no one in them whatsoever, here and there a couple of people sitting with popcorn listening to loud post-disco music blasting from the speakers. There is no band. There are no cheerleaders. The student section is inhabited by about six guys, all of them sitting on their hands looking glumly toward the court, wondering, it appears, why they are here, why they bothered to spend their money for this when there are good beer joints open where they wouldn't have to sit sober for two hours. Out on the court players shoot apathetically at the hoops, wondering what all the ruckus has been about all week, all the hard practices upon their return from Christmas break. It would have been better to have just waited a few more days, maybe next week, and played then. Maybe by then somebody might have possibly given a shit.

"We drove all the way up here for this?" Sammy says. "We'd have done better if we'd just gone somewhere and got hooty."

"I vote we do that," John says. "I for damn sure haven't lost anything here."

"I'm finding a seat," Phillip says. "They're fixing to tip off."

Actually, this turns into a pretty good game. The unknown team from southeast Podunk hustles and scraps and tries everything it can muster to hang with the state university. At the end of the first half they are only behind by four points, and what fans the home team has managed to draw into the arena are growing a tad anxious. John and Sammy still have an itch to leave, John to go somewhere and drink and Sammy to get back to town and have the time to perhaps share his seed with whoever is next on his list, but Phillip is settled in and David doesn't feel like driving back immediately, and since David is driving they sit a while longer. The home team finally gathers itself, and midway through the second half the game becomes a rout, so they head for the exit to go home.

They are about to cross the road to where they parked when they see activity around the van. Sammy quickly breaks into a run and crosses the street in traffic ahead of them, and it takes a moment for everyone left behind to realize what is going on. Someone—or a group of someones—is trying to break into David's van. Actually, they are not trying, but are already inside. The side panel doors are open and the driver's seat is occupied by a figure with his head beneath the dash. Whether the van is merely being rifled or an attempt is being made to steal it makes no difference. No one has to argue against the fact that it's up to them to stop what's happening.

Sammy is way ahead of everyone else and there at the van before the thieves know he is coming. He lowers his shoulder and slams into one guy from behind and sends him hurtling into the open sliding door, where he falls into another guy who's already inside and they both tumble into the floorboard. Sammy doesn't stop but just jumps in to join them.

John gets there next and tries to open the front passenger door, but it is still locked on this side and he can't get in. By this time the fellow on the other side behind the wheel has raised his head and sees John at the opposite window jiggling the handle and his two friends buried in the back under some wild man who's about eight-foot two, and it occurs to him in all this sudden activity that the time of robbery and vandalism he's been engaged in the past few minutes has suddenly come to an abrupt and unforeseen end. He pushes himself out the driver's side door and gets ready to run, but David comes around from the back of the van and grabs his arm while Phillip looks in the side doors to see if Sammy needs any assistance.

He doesn't.

Sammy is a big enough guy for the task he's taken on. He's been a linebacker in high school football way back when and stayed busy since picking up wooden pallets like sofa pillows for years, unloading trucks and pulling heavy pallet jacks like they're loaded with feathers, and so two sorry kids from some local high school pinned down on a seat beneath him is nothing much to worry about. He stays on top of them and holds them down with his left hand and swings his right down like a hammer on their heads and shoulders and the back of their necks. From time to time he thinks about maybe stopping but decides against it.

In the meantime, the jacket sleeve that David has in his grasp slithers off its owner's arm and David stands holding a jacket while the guy in his shirtsleeves runs down to the back of the lot trying to get away. The only problem with that is there is no way to exit the lot from there—a high chain link fence surrounds the lot on three sides—and all there is to do is either attempt to scale the fence in record time or turn around and go back the way he came from, and that's not good either, because now John and David have come up on him and he has two people to go through just to get back to where his buddies are at the moment busy getting the shit kicked out of them. He is not very enamored with his choices.

This is when he remembers he has a knife in his pocket and it might be a good idea to pull it out and let it be known it's there and there's a good chance it might get used. Of course, it's not a machete or a switchblade or anything scary like that; it's mainly a Barlow pocket knife with three blades and a can opener, but he reaches in his jeans to pull it out anyway. He's got his hand in his pocket when David steps forward and clubs him a good one on the side of the head. He doesn't bother thinking about his Barlow any longer, but just decides the best thing to do is go on and fall on the pavement and pretend he's either dead or invisible or this is all just one bad dream and maybe in a while he might wake up from it if he's lucky.

Police lights begin flashing back toward the street and people leaving the game gather around. Two policemen first stop at the van and observe Sammy clubbing his two new acquaintances like baby seals. They ask Phillip, who's standing by with nothing much to do, what's going on.

"It's either a massacre or a bloodbath," Phillip tells them. "I've been standing here trying to figure it out."

They tell Sammy how they're the police and he has to stop what he's doing. Sammy rises up and sees the flashlight in his eyes and makes out the badges on their uniforms. He would like to keep pummeling the two fellows he's sitting on but decides it is probably too much of a good thing and perhaps he should stop. He cuffs one kid a final time on his ear in parting and stands back from the van, his two hands held up in the air to show how compliant and nice a guy he is.

"Hi, officers," he grins. "I thought you'd never get here."

"What's going on?" the short cop asks.

David and John walk up with their arms around their own prisoner, a skinny kid with a Smashing Pumpkins tee shirt on and a trail of blood dripping down his nose. John is smiling, pleased and in sudden awe of the unexpected vicious right hand of David that none of them have previously known he possessed. Everyone looks so goddamned maniacal with their lopsided smirks to Phillip that he feels like it is up to him to explain what is transpiring here to the authorities, otherwise Clarksville may not have a hoosegow large enough to house them all tonight.

"We were at the basketball game," he begins, "and when we came out these three guys were in the process of breaking into our car."

"Ronnie," says one of the cops, looking at the kid with the nosebleed. "What in the hell are you doing here?"

"I don't know," says Ronnie.

"Looks to me like you're about to get in some trouble."

"About?" says John.

"Well," says the tall cop, "we're just at the stage of trying to figure out what's really happening here. You gentlemen say your car was getting broken into, but we know these boys here and it might be they have a different story."

"We was just walking by," says one of Sammy's punching bags, "and these guys started a fight with us."

"Oh, goddamn," says Sammy. "Do I really need to knock the living shit out of you again?"

"Ain't nobody hitting anybody right now," says the short cop. "You just stand right there and keep your distance." He walks up and shines his flashlight in Phillip's face. "Where are you guys from, tell me that."

"Abington," Phillip says.

"You're kind of a long way out of your territory, aren't you?"

"We drove here to see the game," David says.

"That's what we're trying to figure out," says the tall cop, "if you fellows are here to see a basketball game or to maybe get yourselves into a little trouble."

Phillip can see the slant of this game already. It doesn't take a whole lot of detective skills to comprehend how these two cops know these three punks from somewhere, are drinking buddies with their dads or go to church with their families or live next door or might even be related to them, cousins and uncles and such. This is dangerous turf here, he decides. This is exactly the type of situation that can suddenly grow into something entirely distasteful. It's not like he's paranoid or anything like that. He's just seen this kind of shit a few too many times already in his life and doesn't need an encore presentation tonight. Phillip thinks how now is the time to maybe tread a tad softly on this alien ground, and is just about to subtly suggest such a strategy to his pals when Sammy unsurprisingly takes a step forward and plants himself directly in the two policemen's personal proximities.

"Let me lay it out for you so you can get it down right in your report the first time," he says.

"Let us ask the questions," Shorty says.

"How about I just give you the answers, bubba, and then let you take it from there."

Sammy leans forward a little more and the two policemen inch backward slightly. Sammy is, despite his smiling countenance, relatively larger than both of them put together, and despite the fact they have pistols on their hips and clubs sheathed on their belts they are not too happy with the idea of attempting to keep this imposing yet happy character from shooting the breeze.

"Your next of kin here, or whoever these pieces of shit are to you, have jimmied open the door on my friend's van so they could get inside and steal something. We caught them in the act because we left the game early. We kicked their ass for a while until you showed up, and then we stopped. That's the story. Nothing else happened, get it? Now the question is this—are you going to fuck with us because we're not from around here, or are you going to do your goddamn duty and haul these little assholes away from here so we can go home? Hell, we're not fucking stupid, you know. We already know you ain't going to do anything to them. We're just saying okay, they broke in the van and we kicked their butts for it. They didn't get anything and it's not like there's any big damage. We just want to get in the van and go home, so you tell me if you want to make a bigger deal about all this or not."

The two policemen look at each other and the short one tells the three boys to get in the back of the cruiser. Nobody gets cuffed. It's pretty clear that all that's going to happen is they're going to get themselves a free ride home, and at this moment that is fine with John and Phillip and Sammy. It's not fine with David, who will whine and piss and moan about the scratches on his Caravan's door until the end of time, but that is David. David sometimes does not understand the importance of the strategic retreat in the grand scope of things.

"So you don't want to prefer charges?" Shorty says.

"No," Phillip says. "We'd just like to call it a night and go home."

"Okay, maybe that's the right way to go," Shorty says, like he is doing them a big favor and they should be grateful for it. The two policemen are still standing outside their cruiser talking it over with some newly-arrived cops in a second cruiser with the three car burglars stowed away in the back seat when David starts up the van and they drive away.

"Well, I don't know about the rest of you," Sammy says, "but I sure have had fun tonight. There's nothing like some wholesome recreation to make a guy feel good and alive."

"Just think," John says, "it's early yet too. The night is young. Imagine what the evening may have in store for us once we get back to town." He and Phillip pile into the seat by the back window and press their faces against the glass. It's dark and no one can really see them, but they know how this drives David crazy, so that's good enough for right now.

David and Sammy smoke and look out at the highway through the windshield. On the tape player the Moody Blues sing about Knights in White Satin and all sorts of stuff like that. Nobody talks much on the way, and they are back in Abington before they know it.

WEDNESDAY, DECEMBER 28

Phillip is close to being proud of himself when he wakes up, since from his preliminary examination before hitting the floor he seems to be hangover-less. This should not be a surprise to him, since he did not imbibe much at all last night, and, in fact, came directly back to the house when he got back to Abington, opting not to go out for beers with his traveling companions. If he had to tell the truth under oath, he would say he'd not gone because it seemed that the correct thing for him to do was to return to his wife and child and play husband and father a little while and not be so selfish entertaining himself, but the real truth of the matter is he is starting to tire a bit of his friends' company and needs to take a little break.

This is not the first time he's felt this way. Janet's parents still live in Abington, and on Christmas and several other times during the year she always wants to come back to her old neighborhood and move in the old house with her parents for a week or so and visit some, so it's not like Phillip and his friends are ever separated for too very long, either by miles or time or the daily transfigurations of life that tend to multiply and make friends into strangers simply because of a lack of common reference. No, he is still around his old pals enough to keep tabs and not feel like they are all waving at each other from distant planets. Sometimes stories and events get recounted a second time and re-told a different way with certain embellishments not provided before, and it is then that Phillip starts recognizing how during this portion of each current reunion there is nothing much new under the sun for anyone to discover. This is when he realizes how his old friends are beginning to blend in with the way he perceives his new friends apart from Abington in this apex of his middle years, and how the myth of the old days with fabled events and storybook endings are not really lined up in the same order and position in his head anymore. Time, he thinks, changes everything. It's beginning to feel like he's got as little in common with his old friends in about the same way he is with the new acquaintances he deals with every day in his real life away from Abington. He is two hours down the highway, but in either place there seems to be a similar thread, where everyone is somewhere and he is off by himself somewhere else.

He's the first one awake in the house this morning other than Scratchy the cat, who watches him make coffee while sitting at attention by the refrigerator. Scratchy is old and fairly fat, and when he gets up to move from one place to another emits a sound that is a cross between a wheeze and strangulation. It is like a lot of things in this house Phillip finds himself a prisoner of this week, one more thing that's somewhat irritable and annoying to be around. He wishes he could have a better attitude about things, but he knows it's useless. It's hard to think when he thinks he's constantly being watched, by this cat, by his in-laws, by Janet, looked at out of the corner of a whole lot of eyes like he's fixing to do something to upset the scheme of things around here and out in the world.

Janet is up by the time he's into his second cup of coffee. Even though he was home early last night and did his best to be congenial with her parents and his daughter, she is still a little distant first thing this morning. This aloofness, though, is fairly par for the course so far as their marriage has gone these fifteen years—whenever something is chewing at Janet she consistently opts for cheerful silence. This seems to be her way of making some form of peace and not blurting out any rash accusations, unfounded or not.

"Did you sleep okay?" he asks.

"Yes," she says. "Did you?"

"I was all right. I miss my pillow, though. I can't ever seem to get comfortable unless I'm in my own bed."

By nine everyone is up and Janet and her mother get busy fixing breakfast. Melanie runs through the house trying to incite Scratchy into some form of play, but can't seem to provide enough inspiration to get a response. Phillip sits down in the living room with Donald, Janet's dad, and watches him read the morning paper while halfway looking at "Regis and Kathy Lee." The Christmas tree is still standing by the window, and Phillip wonders if he ought to offer to take it down. Probably not. He already gets accused of being grumpy about the holiday season too much, wanting it over as fast as possible. He doesn't need to feed the fodder any and catch whatever ire may be floating around as if it was waiting to alight on his being.

Melanie runs into the living room chasing the cat and veers off track and trips on a table leg and falls into the tree. Ornaments and lights drop from the branches and the tree begins to topple to the right, descending upon Donald and his newspaper and cup of coffee balanced on the arm of his chair. For an instant Phillip thinks maybe he can jump up and catch the tree before it engulfs Donald, but he is too slow in his reflex action and the tree falls and covers Donald like an artificial pine blanket. His coffee cup takes flight and Scratchy screeches and Melanie cries bloody murder. Janet runs from the kitchen and sees how the tree has swooped down and covered her father. She looks at the broken ornaments and un-twinkling lights on the carpet beneath her feet, then looks at Phillip. He looks back at her, sits with his legs crossed and a third cup of coffee balanced on his knee. On the television Bobby McFerrin is singing "Don't Worry, Be Happy" and Kathy Lee Gifford is grinning like she's the happiest she's ever been in her entire life.

"My god," she says. "What in the world is going on?"

"It looks to me like the tree ate your dad," Phillip says, immediately regretting letting this come out of his mouth but knowing there was really no way he could have stopped it.

"Why weren't you watching Melanie? You just let her run wild all the time and this is what always happens."

Ah, he thinks, somehow I knew this would get traced back to me.

The tree moves and Donald's hands appear between the branches, sticking out like fingers from a grave beckoning someone to come closer so they can get themselves dragged into Hell. Phillip wants to sit politely and let Donald get out of this predicament on his own but decides that maybe as head of the visiting household and a prime member of the holiday festivities staff he probably should get up and lend a hand. Melanie is still crying, but at least Scratchy has stopped yowling and wishing to be put out of his misery. Things are looking up. Phillip is hopeful that maybe in a couple of hours life here at Holiday Central can get back to normal.

He untangles the tree from his father-in-law, trying to keep limbs from coming unattached and more decorations going into freefall. He finally gets it propped up over in a corner, but since the stand has disassembled itself into three pieces he has to wedge the tree between the window and a coffee table to keep it from falling again, and then he is afraid to move away from it for fear he hasn't got it totally secured. Maybe if he stands here and holds it until the Epiphany arrives everything will be all right. Donald, though thoroughly pissed, is all right and not close to stroking out, and Melanie is traumatized for the next five minutes until suddenly it is as if nothing has happened for her to have ever been concerned about. Janet goes back into the kitchen with her mother, and Phillip assumes with the low conversation going on out there the discussion is possibly about how pathetic a husband and son-in-law he truly is. He stands by the tree adjusting and affixing balls and lights, trying to be honest enough to see if he should take the blame for all this chaos, destruction, and complete lack of tranquility in his wife's childhood home this morning. He is generally his worst critic, but he just can't see it this time. He was drinking a cup of coffee. He was smiling. He didn't have a hangover. He doesn't see how he can get blamed for too much after all that.

He is glad he's promised Miller he would come help out at the Market this afternoon.

***

It's coming up on noon, and Sammy has seen maybe ten people come through the doors since opening up this morning. Opening time has been pushed back to nine now, since there's no big demand and nothing much left to sell, and for that blessing Sammy is glad, because he truly doesn't think he could have made it in any earlier today. When they'd got back last night it was actually warm enough to ride around some, so he'd taken off down the highway to a dive just outside of Celina. He'd thrown some darts and polished off a few boilermakers before speeding back the forty-five miles to Abington, and when he'd got inside his door and got ready to hit the sack the room was spinning around and the whole wide world was funny as hell. How in the hell did I make it back alive with all the alcohol I drank, he'd wondered? It was such a miracle he'd just collapsed there in the dark like a bag of rocks and rested there snickering about it. It was funny how God seemed to love him so much that He just kept him alive no matter what.

Miller wasn't talking this morning. From past experiences Sammy knew it was probably one of a few things, either stress or worry over closing up the Market this week, or the really good chance troubles with that damn Laurel again, which Miller never talks about whatsoever. Sammy wonders sometimes exactly how long Miller has been carrying on with Laurel; it is hard to put a time on it. All Sammy knows is it has been quite a while, a decade at least. He knows that Miller was out of school for good and working six days a week along with him, and this eternal affair was kicking in maybe even before Phillip and John ever got married. David, of course, was married too around then, but was it number one or two of his ex-wives? Sammy tries to remember if he had also been married before Laurel first showed up, but that was a long time ago and his marriage hadn't lasted too very long at all and he'd done his best since then to repress it and forget every damned little detail about what happened in it, the who, what, where and whys. He hadn't been a very good husband and Vickie had been even a worse wife.

If that was possible.

When it's quiet like this, even in the middle of the day with the sun shining and all the traffic going by outside, it's easy to remember and to visualize people and stuff that's happened down through the years since he first started working here. Sammy stands by the front door and looks across at the bread rack in the far corner. He sees the plexiglass borders with the lights inside them and thinks about how it was Miller who stood on the top rung of a ladder trying to fasten the fixtures in place and get the fluorescent lights working, and how he had walked by in the midst of the process and jiggled the ladder only a tiny bit, just in fun, and Miller had gone into a cursing fit because he thought he was about to fall and be maimed forever. He'd gone three days without speaking to Sammy then, and when he'd finally opened his mouth to say anything it was just to intone, "Fuck you."

There had been shoplifters and fights between employees and customers, and one night John had come back into the stockroom and motioned for him to follow him out onto the aisles. They walked up the canned good aisle and a woman was squatted taking a crap in front of the green beans. They'd looked at each other and silently turned around and disappeared back into the store. Damned if it was going to be either one of them who stopped her.

People got fired for stealing. One time the cops came in and took the head butcher away in handcuffs for poisoning his neighbor's dog. The dog kept him up at night, and Ned—that was the butcher's name—liked to get in early in the mornings. He couldn't get enough sleep, so he slipped the mutt rat poison in some hamburger. That was a long time ago too, Sammy thinks. He wasn't sure if Laurel was here by then either.

(There was this kid named Bennie who worked back in Produce. Always ran his mouth and thought he knew everything. Phillip didn't like him worth a shit, and one Sunday afternoon, when Bennie walked up in a salvage trailer to stack an empty pallet, Phillip just nonchalantly walked over and pulled the sliding door down behind him, locked the door in place and walked back up front. This was early afternoon in the middle of summer. It was hot as hell back on the dock, even hotter in the trailers. We could hear Bennie beating on the doors and yelling for somebody *to let him out. I went out on the floor and filled the milk and eggs. Miller stayed up in the office. David and John and Phillip hung out up front bagging and checking. The store was closing at six and we thought about leaving Bennie back there all night, but finally at five-thirty I went back and let him out. He was madder than hell but he didn't want to fight me. He was so chicken-shit he didn't want to get in a fight with anybody. We were pretty sure he'd go tell on us and get us all fired, but he never did. I guess he thought we'd kill him if he went that far. He just shut up after that and worked another couple of years and was all right from then on until he finally moved away. Guess he was afraid we might lock him up again.)*

Sammy doesn't know what became of old Bennie. It was like it was with a lot of folks. They just disappeared.

He thinks again of Laurel and Miller and wonders how many in-store romances he has had himself over the years inside these old walls. There have been girls who ran the registers up front and sales reps who've come in the store wanting shelf allocation and Judy

Mason back in the meat department whose husband had once come in the store looking for him with a pistol in his pocket, and it was a damn good thing Sammy had been off that day or maybe he might be dead right now.

He thinks of all those women and he has to admit he's been lucky as all get-out. He's had a charmed damned life so far. God must definitely love him.

Speaking of sales rep fraternizing, he sees a white Ford pull up and the R.J. Reynolds cigarette representative get out. This is Inez, who's been coming in the Market for a while now, fifteen years maybe, and she and Sammy have spent a lot of time together during that time. He does mean together. Inez may be ten years older than Sammy, but that never stopped anything when he was back in his twenties, and he's thirty-eight now and he still doesn't feel any different about it. Inez is well-preserved, knows it, and knows how to make it work for her. She's fakey as hell with her laughing and flirting and blinking eyes, but when it comes down to it she'll hop in the sack with somebody in the blink of one of those twinkling eyes, especially if she takes a liking to somebody, and it didn't take her long to determine she liked Sammy just fine. I like tall men, she'd told him right from the start. Tall men can wrap around you like a big old snake.

"I thought I'd make one last visit over here and see if I have any product left," Inez tells him. "If I do, I think I'll just pick it up now and take it on over to the new place. Might as well kill two birds with one stone."

"Hell, I thought you were coming in to see me," Sammy says. "I was getting my hopes up."

"Why of course I'm coming to see you, Sugar." Inez does her eye-blinking routine and plants her artificial smile on her face. She has lipstick layered on about a foot deep, and for some reason Sammy seems to find this overabundance of gloss halfway attractive. "You don't think I was going to come over to this section of town and not drop in to say hello to you, do you?"

Sammy rolls the big cigarette rack out so Inez can get behind it and see if she has any inventory in boxes that aren't on the rack. Sammy follows her in behind, and for a moment their hands run up and down each other, and Sammy feels like kissing her right there behind the rack, maybe getting lipstick smeared all over his face or something stupid like that. At the new store he knows there are going to be cameras watching him and everybody else's every little move night and day, but this is the old store and nothing like that exists around here. As long as you're careful you can get away with about anything in this place. He knows. He's done it. And not just once, either. Lots of times. Once again he thinks how he is going to miss this place.

Miller and John are two aisles over boxing up the general merchandise section—can openers, corkscrews, hammers, extension cords—so he shouts to them that he's going to the back for a minute. He hears John answer okay, and he takes his hand and nudges Inez back down the health and beauty aid aisle. She takes her hand and tugs on his belt buckle a little, showing him her teeth and red lips and batting eyes, and all at once he doesn't care whatsoever that she is inching fifty and he is supposed to be working and what might possibly go down if he happens to get caught at what he knows he is fixing to do. He is just suddenly in this reoccurring I-don't-give-a-shit mode he keeps falling into all too frequently lately, all the time, really, if anybody wants to get technical, and he's going to go ahead and do what he wants to do right now and if God shoots him down with a thunderbolt later on, well, so be it. He'll have fun while it lasts and maybe it will be worth it in the end, and if it isn't, well, he's been fucked up before and this probably won't be the last time either.

They go through the swinging doors into the stockroom and go down a small flight of steps. They stop in the middle because of this big long sloppy kiss they're sharing so they won't trip and fall down into the hallway, then they get to the bottom and go inside a door to the small break room that only about three people ever use. There's a small plastic-covered divan against the wall that Sammy thinks they might be able to both inhabit for however long it takes, and the next thing he knows is he is shedding clothes and helping Inez shed hers too and then they are naked and against each other and oh my oh my, he thinks, but this woman certainly knows how to screw.

He tells her so and she says the feeling is mutual.

"Hey, Sammy!"

He hears Miller yelling for him up in the stockroom and he puts a finger to his lips to tell Inez to be quiet. Probably Miller is sick of watching the front end even if there's nobody up there and is wondering what in the hell Sammy is doing. The light is off in the break room, but there's a small light from the adjoining restroom, so Sammy and Inez can see each other. This is not good, because every time they look at each other they start laughing, and they are afraid Miller is going to hear them. At least the door is locked, so he can't come barging in, but if he knows they're in here, he's probably not going to go away.

The knob jiggles and fists start banging on the door.

"I know you're in there, goddamit!" Miller says. "John saw you heading back this way." The door gets pounded again. "You're an asshole, you know it? I'm damned if I'm going to stand up front all day while you're back here screwing your ass off. I've got stuff to do."

"Let it ride, baby." Sammy says. "It don't matter what happens around here anymore. Who gives a shit? Might as well have some fun."

"You're not Cyndi Lauper, goddamn it."

"Maybe I am," Sammy says. "Maybe I'm so traumatized by the store closing down I'm having an identity crisis."

"Hurry up and get back up front," Miller says. "I don't have all day." They hear him shuffle up the stairs and the swinging door creak as he goes back out on the floor.

"I guess you'd better get back," Inez says, "or you're going to get in trouble."

"I'm going back," Sammy says, "but my break's not over with yet." He positions himself on the tiny couch again, wiggles to make himself fit. "I've still got a couple of minutes left."

Inez starts laughing again and her eyes open and close like a poker machine that's just hit the jackpot.

***

Miller still hasn't spoken to him by the time they close up at five, but as they get ready to leave Sammy puts his arms around Miller and John and gives them his famous bear hug.

"You fellows are all too damned serious. Ya'll are going to die of a heart attack if you don't lighten up a little."

"You're the one who's going to have the damn stroke," Miller says. "You don't know when to stop. You never have."

"I can't help it if all the women in the world want me," Sammy grins, "now, can I? What do you want me to do? Tell all these women no? Does that sound like Sammy Garrison to you? I don't know about you boys, but if I'm not screwing somebody when I get the chance you'd better check my pulse, because I might be dead without anybody knowing about it. No, the problem ain't me, guys, it's you. You boys are wasting your lives being careful, worrying about what's going to happen, if you're going to get in trouble or die or something. You just need to say fuck it and be like yours truly. Get your rocks off now before you get so old all you can do is think about it. You ain't ever going to see me crying about what might have been and what I should have done."

"Yeah, well you're like Elvis," John says. "If you can't find a partner you just go ahead and use a wooden chair."

"I've had worse ideas," Sammy says. "You know me, I'd screw a black mamba if I had the chance."

"Only," Miller smiles, "if one of us was around to hold its damn head for you."

***

Everyone joins forces later at Dino's to eat greasy cheeseburgers and drink draft beer until midnight.

Even though it has been spring-like during the afternoon, the weather is turning colder with the night and spits of unexpected snow trail by the window beneath the restaurant lights. Christmas is over but somehow they know Old Bing is still singing and the season isn't quite done yet.

"Three more days to go," Miller says. "I can use all the help I can get from here on out. Everything gets reduced to rock bottom starting tomorrow, so there are actually going to be people coming in to buy what's left. I heard an advertisement on the radio coming over here. Believe it or not, Jim is sending me a couple of checkers over in the morning to man the registers, but I can use more help if all you guys will show up." He looks over at Sammy and shakes his head. "I can use you too, you damn knucklehead, if you can manage to keep your damn pants on." "You can count on me, boss," Sammy grins. "I'll be by for a couple of hours in the morning," says David, "but I have to be at work at noon, so it won't be long."

"I'm in for all three days," John says, "just for old time's sake, though. I'm not busting my ass to make it go smooth for good old Jimmy and the new Overton's."

"I'll be there every day too." Phillip holds a mug up at everyone and winks. "I'll probably end up getting divorced because I spend more time with you guys and the Market, but so be it. Everybody else is divorced— why should I be the Lone Ranger?"

"That's it, then," Miller says. "It's all hands on deck. Three more days and then it's say hello to the future." It comes to him that he's drunk. He's been downing drafts like there's no tomorrow when there's still actually a couple of sunrise sunsets left in his future. It comes to him that he's had a whole lot of beer tonight, maybe more than his quota, which he has to admit, is way up there. What do you know, he thinks. Me drunk. Who would have ever thought such a thing could happen?

THURSDAY, DECEMBER 29

Miller doesn't get his accustomed alone time in the store this morning, because when he pulls into the lot David is sitting on the curb outside waiting for him. In a perfect world Miller would be pleased to see some enlisted help already on hand on what promises to be a booger of a day, but because he has a hangover and his head is splitting he would have preferred having a few minutes alone to gather himself before the onslaught of human voices ringing in his ears began again. The fact that it is tee-totaler non-drug using David in his sights this moment doesn't set well with his faculties much either. David has never had any sympathy for anyone when it comes to the after effects of the revels of the night before, always seeming to take a perverse pleasure in rubbing it in to the suffering party before him and continually mentioning how he is feeling fine while they are hovering near death and consistently doing his best to compound the misery in whatever way possible.

He is doing it now, already, as Miller walks up to unlock the doors.

"I thought for a while I was going to be the only survivor from last night, and how it would be just my rotten luck to be the only one here to face the masses this morning. But I had faith in you, Miller. I knew you'd come dragging in somehow and make an appearance, even if you are too hungover to do any actual work."

"It's an hour until opening."

"Yes, but there's so much to do. The workload is overwhelming. Isn't that what you were saying last night?"

"To tell you the truth, Davey boy, I don't really recall a whole hell of a lot that was discussed last night."

"Well, then, you didn't miss anything."

In his annoying way, David is right. There isn't really too much to do around this ghost store this early in the morning. Miller doesn't have to do books or run checks or count money anymore but just bags everything up in a locked bag and he or Sammy runs it over to the new store later so they can fool with it there. The new store's books are all jived with a fancy big ass processor that's connected to everything here at the old store, so they simply take the delivery and add it up and count it and store it and act like they are the ones who collected it there at the new store, which will be a hundred percent true in a few days but is nowhere near reality now. Right this instant the old store is open and the new one isn't, only one is actually taking in any money, and this more or less justifies the attitude Miller feels that keeps coursing through his veins, which is screw all the damn Overtons and their crew and the pitiful-ass ponies they all rode in on for acting like they're doing anything worthwhile whatsoever.

No talking or sightings of Bill this early morning, not with David around breaking the sacred privacy, and Miller wonders if in the three mornings left he will ever feel the presence of Bill again. There are a lot of things like this he is beginning to sense, customers who come and go he has seen for years that he wonders now if they will matriculate over to the new store or migrate and go somewhere else, vendors, delivery people, truck drivers, route salesmen, everything and everyone going by his sight and proximity for what could possibly be the last time. If he said something about it out loud, people within hearing distance will gather that he thinks the world is ending, dying a slow death like Ava Gardner and Gregory Peck did in *On the Beach*. It is a lot like that, he thinks, radiation poisoning or taking a death-inducing capsule or a bomb dropped and that's it. It's done, life going out gasping its last breath and never being the same again. Too bad he doesn't have a dish like old Ava around to kiss goodbye while all this end shit is coming on.

He opens the safe and puts tills out in all five lanes, does it the way he always has even if he probably isn't going to have enough checkers around today to open them all. He's got two part-timers from the new store who are generally worthless—which is probably why Jim is lending them out to him in the first place--and just possibly might not even show up, and there's him and Sammy, and maybe Phillip in a pinch. It's been a while since he ran a register, but Miller bets Phillip hasn't forgotten a thing. David and John are other matters. They probably remember how but will act like they've totally forgotten what to do. That's the way they were when they worked at the Market back in high school and college days, preferring always to do something else other than get marooned in a check lane, and Miller doesn't see any reason why anything should be different now. Some things are eternal, he tells himself.

Sammy cruises in five minutes before opening. It doesn't make much difference him coming in at this time instead of earlier, because it's not like the back door has to be opened for any deliveries or anything.

Milk and bread, skeleton deliveries, that's all that's coming in, and today's the last day for even that to happen. The orders are so ridiculously small they can come through the front door and get checked in up front. Sammy gets rid of the waiting deliveries in about two minutes flat, signs his name on the order pads and takes his copies, and just like that the incoming delivery history of old Overton's Market is finished. Miller marks the occasion silently, wondering if anyone but him knows something has passed, something has ended.

"Seems weird to not have to go back and start unloading a grocery truck this morning," Sammy says. "I don't know how to act not busting my ass right off the bat on a Thursday morning."

Miller switches on the automatic doors and customers begin trickling in. The number is not enough to go into a frenzy and full-scale panic about, but there are more people in the store fifteen minutes after opening this morning than there have been in a while, when all the stock first began to dwindle and service started getting scant, and Miller knows it won't take many more customers coming in for him and his makeshift staff to be totally outnumbered.

But, ah, he is used to that. He knows all about being outnumbered, being up against the odds, having to fight to make it through another day. He's seen and lived through so many complications and continuing dilemmas through all the years here inside these walls that not a thing is going to faze him or defeat him now. He's arrived at the point that when he sees trouble coming he tends to smile and welcome it. Let his fellow employees call out sick for their shifts. Bring on impending snow scares and blizzards and widespread panic. Throw in Christmas and Thanksgiving and all the other major holidays where feasts and barbecues have to be observed. Send them all at him in continuous wave and thrusts. He looks forward to the challenges. He can negotiate a hopeless fight into his own victory. He is welcome to whatever slings, arrows, and assorted ammunition decide to hurtle his way.

This means he's crazy. He knows that too. He is good with such a diagnosis. Soon customers are streaming in and out the doors and cluttering up the aisles just like this is a regular shopping day back in the good old not so distant past. Sammy sees the people and for a little bit, if he didn't know better, can imagine it's the beginning of the holiday season all over again. If he could find some station still playing Christmas music he could play it on the intercom and it would be just like last week. But Christmas is over, there is no more music and the decorations are boxed up now, sent over to the new store to be glanced at and no doubt immediately thrown away, and this scene before him is but a last gasp gesture by these shoppers to say goodbye to the old place by searching for some kind of bargain that is never going to come their way again.

Everything is half price the next three days. Sammy supposes that is bargain enough, if only there was anything much left on the shelves to buy. But he knows people. He's seen them in action plenty of times. They'll buy a coffee can full of dead kittens if they think they are getting a deal on it.

Take old Alvin Reed just coming in the door. How many years has this old buzzard run a barbecue stand down the road? How many mornings has he come in here before he opens up, looking for, what he calls them, good bargains, which translated means dented cans and squashed bread and boxes with torn openings that nobody's ever going to buy. Nobody but him, that is. You can find a bag of sugar with a hole in it and an army of ants trying to cart it off and he'll snatch it up in a second, put it in his bascart and come looking for somebody to mark it down for him. Alvin likes broken eggs and leaking bottles and anything with sticky goo all over it. Miller swears he comes in and destroys stuff over in the aisles when he thinks no one is looking so he can get the price reduced, and Sammy wouldn't bet against that theory. But the strange thing is Alvin's barbecue is pretty damn good when it comes down to it. If you can forget about all the crappy merchandise he wheels and deals with and carts out the door, when you go over to his place and have a sandwich you have to admit it goes down pretty damn fine. Alvin always gives Miller and Sammy two sandwiches for the price of one, throws in some out of date potato chips, and slips in a beer when no one is around to see him doing it, even though Alvin hasn't got a license to sell beer and never would think of getting one because it might cost him a little money. It's been a lot of years Sammy and Miller have been getting out of the store for a while and dropping by Alvin's for a long mid-afternoon lunch, coming back tanked to the gills with uplifted spirits and a whole joyous and refreshed way of viewing the remainder of their shifts.

One good thing about Overton's is you could get away with stuff like that after you'd been around a while, and Miller and Sammy qualified in the longevity category.

Miller puts David to work making sure the milk and eggs are as full as they can get, mainly to shut David up and provide himself with a little peace, and he goes ahead and mans the register until John and Phillip come in together. By ten the two borrowed checkers are clocked in and assigned lanes, and Miller is free to look around and do whatever job that needs his attention. This is like his job description, what he's been doing for two decades and more at Overton's Market, so it is not really like work to him anymore; it is simply what he does, what he knows he is damn good at. There is a gnawing suspicion in him that this may be one of the talents he possesses that may soon not be needed anymore. At the new store there may be no place for his kind of expertise.

***

It sounds stupid, but Phillip finds running a cash register about as rewarding as anything he's ever done in his life, even teaching. There is something about the way he can immerse himself in numbers and times and statistics while checking and performing transactions that keeps him involved and tuned in to the moment much more than going over events in United States history which always seem to emerge as tired words out in the air that no one much wants to hear, much less retain. He can add three totals together and divide it by three and get an average amount of purchase, keep doing it and building on it until all the pertinent numbers and averages and figures are stored like a database in his head, and when he snaps back to the real world it is like he has been on a trip through time and space and past the stars, and now that he has returned it is his secret alone to harbor, and it is his thing only, and none of the world will ever know what he has done or where he has been in the far-reaching scope of his roving brain.

So Phillip is happy to jump in a check lane and meet the onrushing crowds, to rush them through and add their numbers up in the glorious swirl of his mind.

It is like a free excursion into the past, when he worked with friends and all was cut and dried and he wasn't surrounded by a roomful of people who didn't give the first happy shit about what he had to say.

There is just so much milk and eggs to fill the coolers with, and when the stock is all out David comes back up to the front end and helps John bag groceries. Sacking up orders reminds him of when they all first started, how he and John and Phillip and Sammy and Miller were all a bunch of goofy teenagers on their first job, anxious to do well and not get fired, showing up on time with dreams of upcoming paychecks to buy clothes and cars and food with and not having to ask anyone for it, to not have to wait for it or be patient and have it given to them. He almost hates to have to leave in the next hour to go to damn Abington Home and Hardware, his real job now in these days of adulthood, because it's all so here and now there, it's not like it is here, something remembered you still have occasion to smile about. There's not too awful much out in the world now like the Market is and always has been, not that David can see.

John bags orders and thinks of how much money he used to make here on this front end in tips, how he would try to make sure he was the last one in on Friday afternoons and Saturdays so the odds would increase that everybody in front of him would get assigned to a check lane and after they were all taken up he would then be free to bag. He could go out into the lot pushing the customers' groceries in a cart, sometimes two carts with his left forearm pushing the lead one and his right hand pulling the second, and he would plant his toe beneath the wheel when he was on the hill or lean the front against the car door while he loaded the groceries. Heavy items, soda, dog food in the floor, milk and eggs wedged in on the seat, build a little safety fortress around them so they wouldn't slide off and get broken and mashed. Sometimes there were dogs in the car barking and snapping at him. He remembers a time when he opened the back door of a car and a female lion sat there looking at him. Thought it was Elsa from "Born Free", he thinks, scared the shit out of me. Another time he kept walking by a car on a Friday night and seeing the same guy asleep behind the steering wheel. After a couple of hours he finally went up and looked through the glass. Wondered what to do, then finally went inside and told the co-manager, who went outside and took a look himself, then came back in and called the cops. The guy was dead, bought the frigging farm before he had time to come inside and shop

Creeped me out for a while, John thinks. First time I'd ever seen a dead guy outside of a funeral home.

As fast as Miller is on the register, he doesn't really think he's going to need to open all five lanes at once today, even if he is lucky enough to have that many bodies to run them. There is just so much merchandise people can buy in this store on this Thursday and the next two days; whatever is going out the door this moment and the next is not being replaced, so with a steady stream of hands taking items off the shelves it stands to reason that becoming empty is the next state of affairs for Overton's Market. Get it now, folks, he thinks, because once you don't see it before you there's no reason to wait until next time because it's not going to be there, and the next time you look there won't be anything there at all. Poof. Vanished. He is almost ready to enter into a mode of relaxation when a woman's face appears at the office window. She is not there for any particular business, he can tell that right off the bat. She doesn't need to cash a check or buy a money order or anything routine like that. Miller has been around long enough to know the arrival of trouble when it first appears before him. This looks like just such a case to him from the onset, and he is seldom wrong these days.

"Why do you not have any meat back in your case?" the woman asks. She emphasizes each word in the sentence like she wants to make certain every vowel and syllable is heard clearly, so there can be no beating around the bush so as to not give her a definite answer. "It seems very strange to me to have a sign that says Meat Department and there be nothing of the sort back there for anyone to buy. If someone wanted to be a stickler, they could have a good case in charging you and your business with false advertising."

"It's a sign, ma'am," Miller says. "It's not an advertisement for anything." "Most grocery stores I shop in have fresh meats and produce available for their customers, regardless of their circumstances. I really don't see much of a reason for a store to even attempt to be open if it can't offer any of those services."

"Most stores you shop in aren't closing down in three days. We are. There's a sign on the door that says so—been there for weeks now. It mentions how we apologize for stock levels being low but all the inventory has to be gone by Saturday. That's why everything is fifty percent off, so we can get rid of it."

"That's not doing much to help me out right now, if you'd care to give it a little thought. Fifty percent off of nothing still adds up to nothing for me to buy."

It is not like this lady is old and irrational and around the bend or anything. Hell, she doesn't look like she's that much older than Miller is, ten years tops, but it's pretty obvious she probably doesn't have anything else going on in her life right now to bitch or worry about, so Miller knows he's not going to get rid of her so fast.

"I could go out and kill a chicken for you if you've got a couple of free minutes to wait," he says. He can't help it, the words just escape his lips like they've been plotting a breakout for months. "I'd rustle a cow and cut you up some steaks but I went off this morning without my lariat, and my prize pony has just recently come up lame and had to be shot."

"You don't know who I am, do you?" she says. She acts like she is the possessor of some great secret and quite an abundant supply of ammunition to use against him and cut him down to size, like maybe she is the reincarnation of Mary, Queen of Scots, set loose here in Abington these last days of the year and looking to maybe lope a head or two off to relieve the tedium.

"No, ma'am, I don't know who you are," Miller grins, "and, guess what, I don't really care to find out either."

"My name is Brenda Howell," the woman says victoriously, like she has four aces and two more up her sleeve just in case and he's in deep shit now and ought to have sense enough to know it. "I'm the councilwoman of this district."

"Well then, 'I *am Lazarus, come back from the dead,*'" Miller says, quoting a little T.S. Eliot he has somehow managed to retain from his lost years in college, "'*come back to tell you all. I shall tell you all.*' I was dead and resting in peace until you showed up,

Miss Councilwoman, but you've somehow managed to make me turn over in my grave and twitch around some. That takes a lot of doing on your part to disturb the stone-cold dead so. Spoils the whole notion of resting in peace."

"You're an awfully smart son of a bitch, aren't you?" she says.

"I don't know. I haven't thought about it much. Maybe you ought to go down to City Chambers and take a vote on it. Maybe put forth a little resolution denoting yes or no."

Brenda Howell is about to pitch a real fit and conniption and go public about it, but right then Sammy walks up beside her at the window, leans his elbows on the ledge, and grins at her.

"You forgot some of your shopping items back in Aisle Six," he says. "I gathered them all up from where you left them back behind the corn flakes and brought them up here before you left. I'd hate like hell for you to get home without all your medication."

Sammy spreads out a couple of packages of Contac on the counter, some Tylenol and Sominex, three boxes of sinus tablets. Miller wonders if there's anything left back on the health and beauty aid shelves.

"None of that is mine," she says.

"Well, now, you're right about that," Sammy says. "It's not. All of this belongs to Overton's Market. This pile of stuff is worth a good bit of dough right here, though. That's why I got a little concerned when I saw you back in the aisle trying to stuff it down into your purse."

"I did no such thing."

"Oh, yeah. You did. And then you saw me, and you knew I saw what you were doing, so you took off for another aisle and dumped it out behind the damn Wheaties. I watched you do that too."

"My guess is that's why you're so concerned with us not having any meat in the case," Miller deduces. "I'm betting you thought if you came up here and started raising hell about something you might just be able to walk out the door without anybody saying anything to you."

Councilwoman Howell is at once silent and doesn't seem to want to pursue the subject of the empty meat department anymore. She looks at the items on the counter before her without raising her eyes.

"Usually," Miller says, "when we catch somebody shoplifting we just make them pay for what they took and then tell them never to come back in the store again, but the way I see it, you probably don't have the dough to pay for this crap right now, otherwise you wouldn't have tried to take it in the first place. It's either that or you just love the thrill of committing a crime and trying to get away with it."

"I don't have the money," she says, her voice so low Miller can hardly hear her. "You can believe that or not. I could write you a check, but it would bounce."

"It's four days after Christmas," Miller says. "Technically, this is still the holiday season. So here's a little late Christmas gift for you. Right over there is the door. See where it says Out? My suggestion is you take that sign to heart. Go get in your car and go home and don't come back in here ever again. We close this place in three days, so that shouldn't be that hard to do. How's that qualify as the gift that keeps on giving?"

Brenda Howell looks at Miller and decides not to argue or answer or anything and starts to leave before he and Sammy change their minds.

"Hey," Sammy says. "One more thing." He blocks her path to the door so she can't get around him just yet. "I thought I'd let you know," he smiles. "I'm probably not going to be voting for you come the next election."

***

Even from his check lane farthest from the front office, Phillip has been able to follow along with the drama of the lady shoplifting suspect and how Miller and Sammy handled the situation without missing much of a beat. He has to hand it to them as to how smoothly this incident has gone down; as far as he can tell, other than him keeping tabs on it while it was happening no one else in the store knew anything was transpiring at all. He remembers times in the past where there was a lot of yelling and grappling and bodies rolling around on the floor, and this is a lot different. There was even a Friday afternoon when a shoplifter ran out the door with steaks stuffed in his jeans and darted out into the rush hour traffic and ended up getting splattered by a pickup truck. An ambulance came and took him away and he died a few days later. It was in the papers for a day or two. Here, nothing happened at all. So that's progress, he guesses.

There is a surge of customers to the front to check out—the Herd Instinct, Phillip recalls, they see one move in a certain direction and they all have to follow—and then all at once it is still and quiet once more and he and the two borrowed checkers stand looking at each other. David has to go to work at AHH and John heads to the back to take a smoke with

Sammy, so rather than stand here and attempt to have a conversation with two people he doesn't know, he decides he'll step out on the front walk and take a deep breath of fresh air. What rush there has been has subsided for another interval, maybe even for good this time, and it's quiet outside just like it is inside the store, and in his mind it is like this is an omen of something, a momentary sound of silence, perhaps the calm before an approaching storm. He does not know why he feels this way, but he does. It is a familiar way of being with him. He has always been this way with just about everything in life, sees it coming and going and has to stop and take notice of it somehow.

He takes five minutes on the walk and comes back inside to man his register again. He was up and gone early this morning, and he knows he should call Janet and tell her where he is and how long he'll be here, but he just can't bring himself to do it just yet. He recognizes how he is getting distant and detached from his wife and child a little more each day, but he doesn't quite know how to classify that feeling. He doesn't think the separation involves just he and her—he is fairly certain it is everyone and everything too, the entire enchilada of the world, which is not really a good sign going forward.

Out of the corner of his eye he sees a familiar figure back in the last aisle. The person is studying the contents in the frozen juice cooler, rummaging through cans of orange juice and frozen toppings like maybe there is something valuable hidden away there. She closes the freezer door and starts to walk away, then stops and reaches back inside and extracts some Minute Maid, looks at it as if she might be given a test on its contents later, and then puts it in her cart and shuts the door again and walks toward the front.

It is Betsy. Phillip would recognize her anywhere. It is not that it has been so long since he has seen her or that she has changed so much over the course of twenty years, but it is simply that sometimes a person's face remains permanently fixed in someone's head and it is impossible to remove it entirely. It is not so much love or obsession that keeps it there, but sometimes it is all just a matter of time and circumstance, the power of remembrance, and good old-fashioned fate.

Betsy was a Tabor then but is a Reed now. At least Miller thinks she is a Reed, although he has not heard of her or from her in so many years now that anything could have happened as far as marital status is concerned. Betsy could have a whole string of surnames attached to her profile by now, and he would be one of the last persons on the face of the earth to know about it. Even though they both inhabit the same city at certain points in time and presumably go to the same places at one time or another, it has still been a while since he has seen or heard of her, and he presumes the knowledge is mutual. He does not frequent reunions or keep up with anyone's whereabouts much, and it is not like he and Betsy have doted on each other over the years and made any sort of effort to keep in touch.

He gets to work checking an order out, cans and cans of butter beans, sugar and flour and bottles of ketchup—he wonders if there is anything left back in the aisles—and keeps his head down and leaves it up to God as to whether Betsy the former Tabor who is maybe still a Reed will come through his lane or not. It is funny how in his mind and some far corner of his imagination he is beginning to feel a sort of excitement welling up in him, some long-dormant exhilaration sniffing around for some way to escape and speed the process up a little, get whatever thrilling drama there is outside in the world started and underway once more. Phillip knows how stupid and fruitless this kind of mindset is, how it has so many times betrayed him as a boy and a young man, but it is there all right, still around, and, like all the times before, it is almost impossible to ignore. One would think, he ponders, that a fellow his age with all his years of experience and learned knowledge under his belt might know that emotional and mental gyrations such as this positively never live up to exotic intoxicating far-flung expectations—never have and never will—yet here he goes again. I thought I had grown up and was incapable of random foolishness like this, he muses, but it looks like I was thinking in a smoky room and couldn't see the truth too clearly. It appears I gave myself too much credit for being smart and mature and entering smoothly and wisely into my role as a mature adult, and here it is now with the writing on the wall for me to read, and I am dead wrong once more.

And the sad thing is he is not surprised in the least way.

He checks out four orders as fast as he can, doing his best to stay busy and allow whatever is going to happen to go ahead and run its course. All at once his line is empty. He looks up and sees that Betsy—who is possibly still a Reed but could be something else—is in another check lane with one of the borrowed checkers, and all at once the old schoolyard feeling of rejection washes over him like a sudden unexpected tsunami, and all the old and ancient feelings of inadequacy and despair over the quicksand of romantic social status envelops him almost exactly as it once had all those years before. He is startled by its resurgent clarity, its dominance of lacking any common-sense qualities he may have learned from experience, how quickly he is right back in the throes of angst and dread and fear, all for the sake of a desire to be wanted or remembered somehow, in some way or another. It is strange how all this unpleasantness is not only not behind him but so readily present in the here and now, and he wonders if it has ever really left him, if it is actually always around biding its time until the moment comes when it can take control of him again. He is not sure if Betsy has seen him and has wisely chosen to go to another lane to avoid any ritual of recognition. He tells himself how the smartest thing he could do at this juncture is stand behind his cash register and wait for the next customer to walk in and begin unloading their cart on the conveyor belt. He could also slip off and make a trip to the restroom, take a moment there in the back, then return to the front and Betsy would be gone. He could get through the day and not have to worry about running into her again for maybe another ten years—twenty if he is lucky—and by that time he will be too old for any of it to matter, or dead and gone or eaten up by dementia and unable to remember any of the worrisome past or who possibly might have been a part of it.

All this gallops through his mind while he walks over to the next lane and begins to bag up Betsy whatever-her-name-is-now's groceries.

"Hello, Betsy," he says.

She looks up and sees him. A veil seems to suddenly be lifted from her eyes, and a smile comes to her face. Phillip doesn't know if she is faking it or not, but the smile is at least better than a frown or a look of bewilderment because she doesn't remember who he is. Maybe things between the two of them never transpired in quite a storybook fashion, he understands that perfectly, but she at least recognizes him and knows his name and has not obliterated him from her psyche completely, so there is, at least, that. These days even the smallest wonders he finds himself being grateful for, gushing from the attention bestowed upon him like a rescued puppy.

"Well, Phillip," she says. "It's you. I didn't know you were still working here."

"Just for a week. Came back to help close the old place down."

"Yes. I saw the ad in the paper and thought I'd come and see what I could find." She motions toward the small order he's bagging. "There's not really that much left to buy, or at least not what I need." She hands the cashier a check and waits for her receipt, glancing back at Phillip and smiling and stuffing the checkbook and pen back into her purse.

"Thank you," says the borrowed cashier. "I'm trying my best not to tell people to hurry back." The cashier laughs like she is Lily Tomlin or somebody. "If they hurry back too fast before the new store opens this place won't have anything left inside it for them to buy anything. It will be a wasted trip."

Betsy doesn't have but one bag, but Phillip picks it up and cradles it in his arms.

"I'll get this for you," he says.

He doesn't know why he's doing such a thing. It is not like Betsy is any middle-aged raving beauty or anything. She is basically no different from when he dated her for what was really a short time back in the olden days of high school. She is an older version now of what she always was, simply okay, no more, no less. She walks ahead of him to her car and he looks at the back of her head and her legs and it is as if she is just some woman who came in to shop today and if he did not know her from a time back and remember making out with her a time or two when there was no one else for him to do such a thing with he would not be talking to her this minute, walking behind her like this with a bag in his hand, following her to some monstrosity of a Monte Carlo to place her one bag on the back seat, because she would be just some other vanilla middle-aged female who held no consequence or memory for him. Had he not known her before in the days and nights of life being pumped up to be far more than it truly was he would not be out here in this lot this moment. He would be inside, closing the old store down, putting to bed an ancient dwelling where dreams and fantasies once got talked about and sometimes even came to life.

"That's funny you're still teaching," Betsy is saying, "because I am too. Still at it. This is my fifteenth year of fourth grade. Same school, same classroom, nothing different at all. Well, maybe that's not true," she laughs. "I forgot about how my name has changed a few times. That's what happens when you get divorced once or twice. Everybody has to get to know you all over again."

"You should just not bring it up in conversation. Act like everything's still the same."

"Oh, I've got too many friends at school who know every little thing I do. I couldn't hide anything from them." She jiggles her keys to find the right one. "What about you? Are you still married to Janet, or are you like me, shopping around every five years or so?"

He starts to lie because he senses there is some kind of opportunity here if the right phrases are employed, but it is another one of those things he doesn't want to do even if he's out here practically daring himself and almost ready to talk himself into doing it. He could fill up a notebook with all these situations and mindsets he keeps immersing himself into these days.

"Yep," he says. "Still married. Fifteen years now. Got a six-year-old daughter."

"I bet she's cute."

"Looks like Janet, thank god."

If this is a golden opportunity to be unfaithful he is not all that impressed with it. It is not anywhere near the high-drama smoky dangerous overtone of a noir movie or a steamy novel. It is plain and pseudo-butterscotchy and G-rated as hell with nothing to come away with to think about or even perhaps regret later. As he walks back inside the automatic doors after saying goodbye he feels no guilt for considering another woman on this day. He knows he will not lay awake in the dark this night thinking over what might have been or how things could have been in the regrettable past had he acted differently one way or another. His pulse does not race with excitement over this chance encounter. His heart does not pound with a wild jungle beat. He has five more hours to work until closing, and he is not distracted in the least. If anything, he is mildly disappointed. He is let down by the barren promise of the past, disheartened somewhat because that promise did not bloom then and does not bloom now. Somehow he expected something more from this life. He is a little disappointed that perhaps he didn't know better. He'd always believed he was smarter than that. It was a buried life he had led back then and the life he inhabits today is buried still, and whatever it is down below in the pit of him he fears will never be able to break through what covers him, will never spy the promise of dreams and wishes, all lost to him now because he did not know how to catch them when they appeared to him in those days and nights, could not capture them in the given light until the darkness enveloped him and it was impossible to see where they were anymore.

***

The early afternoon arrives, and what has been a somewhat busy day in spurts begins to trickle down to only a few customers here and there in the aisles. Miller, as a symbolic gesture of finality, has stopped piping in the local oldies station over the intercom as of today, so with the absence of music and human voices the store is quiet and sleepy. John goes down the street to the Dairy Queen for burgers and fries and Miller figures his two borrowed checkers can handle things for a few minutes, so he sneaks off the front to go to the backroom and wolf down a sandwich with everyone else. He is the last one to get there, and he finds John and Sammy sitting on a stack of empty pallets against the wall and Phillip balanced on two plastic milk crates, the three of them eating burgers and fries and drinking Pepsis from the vending machine.

"I'm glad you guys decided not to eat down in the break room," he tells them. "We'd be having to wipe the place down to get rid of our boy Sammy's semen stains. I'd be thinking about him banging some woman down there and end up losing my appetite."

"I'm going to miss this place," says Sammy.

"All you're going to miss is having your little divan downstairs to go to when you feel like laying a little pipe at work," John laughs. "I swear, I get married, get divorced, move away, work for a couple of years, come back into town to visit my parents for Christmas, and not a damned thing has changed one whit around here."

"A little bit," Miller says. "This place is closing. They're opening a new mall next week with a bunch of stores I've never heard of. David hasn't found another dumbass to marry him again. All that's different right there."

"Look at this backroom," Phillip says. "You could stage a circus in here." He gazes around at the expanse of space, the high ceiling, the way the area stretches from one end of the building to the far wall. "Do you guys remember playing basketball and baseball back here at night, sneaking off the front and taking those plastic kick balls and carving out the bottoms of the wooden crates the snap beans came in? We'd hang them up there," he points to the wall above the plastic flaps going into the produce room, "to there," motioning at the entrance to the delivery dock. "We had some damn good games back here too. Play for five minutes or so until we thought somebody was going to miss us, and then run up front and bag, fill up some eggs, spot mop a little, get seen, and then we'd be back here again for the second quarter. Or baseball," he says. "Use the brooms for bats and steal rubber balls off the toy rack."

"The handball games are what I liked the best." Sammy stands up and raises his arm like he is ready to make a serve. "We'd take that rubber ball and pound it off the wall and run all over the damn place. It was great when it was the day before the grocery truck came in, because it was always so empty back here, all the stock worked out and the pallets stacked up and the walls bare. It was like playing in the goddamn Grand

Canyon. Shit, you go over to that new store and there isn't room for anything in that back room. You can't even take a crap anywhere back there without hitting your elbow against something. I'm not looking forward to trying to fit in an entire grocery truck in that dinky little place. Nobody'll be able to even walk through, it'll be so packed."

"What kind of break room have they got over there, Sammy?" John grins. "You checked it out yet?"

"Those days are over with," Miller says. "That's for sure. The place is loaded with cameras. Nobody will be able to pick their nose without it being on film to get looked at and studied later on."

"You know what I say, don't you?" says Sammy. "You can pick your friends, and you can pick your nose, but you can't pick your friend's nose."

"Brilliant," says Phillip. "Why didn't I think of that?"

Miller would stick around longer shooting the shit, but the whole time he's been back here he can't help thinking of something going on out on the floor, up front, maybe out in the parking lot. He doesn't know why it is he's worrying about anything, because it's not like too much of anything terrible is going to happen in ten minutes in an empty store, but he knows how it is with a store—you can take a breath or turn your back, take a day off or even go on vacation for a week, and, sure as hell, something will have happened in the blink of an eye or the thump of a heartbeat, and everything will have changed and will never be the same again. Maybe he is just paranoid. Maybe he is too possessive of this building that feels like it is his but does not have his name on it. Whatever the case, it is hard for him to keep it out of his head for too very

long. It is not like a test that he memorized the answers
to and then forgot. It is not like a woman that he fell
for and suffered because of and then magically got
over it. No, the store is with him all the time. The store
is not like anything else. The store is that thing inside
him that never goes away.

He pushes through the swinging doors with the
porthole windows looking out at the sales floor and
walks up the seventh aisle toward the front, health and
beauty aids to his right, frozen meat and ice cream to
his left. He sees a small puddle of water leaking out
from beneath the popsicles and novelties, and he
knows the case has either kicked off and flipped a
breaker or frozen up and will have to be thawed out.
There's nothing much left to unload or go to ruin in the
cases anyway, and he starts to just ignore it, but then
he thinks of the puddle growing larger and somebody
coming by and slipping and busting their ass and suing
Overton's for negligence or some such shit as that and
it will have all happened on his watch, so he makes an
about face and goes back and grabs a mop and a
yellow sign with Wet Floors printed on it and goes
back, swabs the deck and pats it dry and places the
sign on top of it.

He looks at where the mess was and it is gone. It is
like it was never there. There is nobody, he thinks, who
can clean up a spill better than me. I have been doing
this so long I am the world's best. I went to college
four years and graduated and this is what I'm good at.
This is my claim to fame.

And this is no big shit either, he tells himself. Next
week there will be dirt covering all my handiwork of
the past, this and every inch of every other mess I ever
made clean. It will be like none of it was ever here and
it will be like I didn't clean it up and it will be like

both the spill and me were never present in this place at all.

***

If he thought about it long enough, David is fairly certain he could qualify as one of the biggest dumbasses who ever lived. He has never been his own worst critic before, yet he has no trouble whatsoever envisioning himself this way today, so god knows what the world at large must think of him.

Right now, he stands at his solitary check lane at the front of Abington Home and Hardware. He is the only living cashier on this Thursday after Christmas. There are six more lanes beside him, but for now they sit vacant. The customers who venture in today will have to line up in David's check lane and wait in formation, spell out letters like a marching band, mill together and murmur and gripe about having to stand, and then gaze down at the row of empty registers hoping someone will magically appear and open one of them. The good thing is there is not that much of a chance of there being a long line this day; the aisles are mostly deserted and there are no customers milling around at this point. David wonders why the place is even open when it is like this. Everybody working here should be like everyone else in town and just close down business and working and come back fresh next week to begin the new year.

David is by himself on the front because he is the only front-end employee scheduled at the moment. Everyone else is off. People are out of town for the holidays or busy doing anything but making home improvements, so the company has scheduled accordingly to fit demands. David supposes he should feel lucky to get the extra hours, because if he was back in one of the specialty departments—flooring, painting, appliances, carpentry—he would be the first one to have his hours cut. Since he left Overton's two years ago and started working at AHH he has been assigned to numerous departments as full-time help and subsequently washed out as a failure in all of them. The longest he ever lasted was over in the Gardening Center, where it took them all of three weeks to determine he was an imbecile when it came to stocking and selling. He had no concept of tools or peat moss or any aspect of how to get something to grow, thinking maybe if something had sprouted it was only through a miracle of God. He has at least managed as his greatest accomplishment to not get fired, but instead marks his time getting shifted from department to department with the tagline that maybe the next stop will be the one he is most suited for. After all, he had turned in a sparkling application two years back, had a good resume and a nice reference from Overton's, and had scored high on the testing portion. On paper he had looked like a great hire.

David knows he has always looked good on paper. He had always made straight A's, been on the honor roll, breezed right through college with his BA in Art, but the problem was the same here at AHH as it has always been everywhere—when it came down to cases, he had a lot of information in his head, he could paint pictures and draw sketches, but in the mainstream of the occupational world he has no blessed idea how to fit in.

It wasn't that he disliked being a cashier so much. It was okay. He had done his share of checking back at Overton's, and while running a cash register wasn't like it was anything prestigious to label as your primary occupation, it still paid the bills and made the work shift go by without dragging. Other than slow business days like this one, it was not so bad here at AHH either. The only thing that really bothered him was the fact he was the only male checker in the entire store. All the rest were women. All the better high-paying, rapid advancement positions were manned by men, and there was a good scattering of women making good money and moving up the ladder back in the specialty departments too. But here he was up front, stuck with a bunch of boring females with drab husbands and homely children and the same old average hourly wage that never changed. It was hard to have any pride in his work when he felt like he was the last straw at the bottom of the barrel. Every time he came to work he immediately started feeling that everyone was looking at him and wondering how he ever became so worthless.

The only good thing about being here today is he is up front in a deserted store with nothing to do and Darlene Deason is at the Customer Service and Returns desk by herself, and with no customers to check out and nothing going on in the store except the sound of Bruce Springsteen singing "I'm On Fire" through the speakers, David is free and unencumbered enough to stroll over from his lane and lean on the partition of Darlene's work area and try to initiate some form of conversation with her. Darlene isn't exactly a knockout when it comes down to it; her looks are only slightly elevated from the totally forgettable checkers David generally had to work alongside. She didn't have much to say and had probably never done anything interesting her entire life, but she was thirty and didn't have a harelip or crossed eyes and didn't weigh in at two hundred or more pounds, so she was at least tolerable. David didn't even know if she was married or not and didn't give much of a cheerful shit either way. It wasn't like he was going to ask her out to a movie or anything, wasn't wanting to begin some office romance and end up with a lot of workplace drama on his hands. Hell, he is just bored and wants to talk. It was bound to be better than standing off by himself thinking what a poor miserable fuckoff he'd become in his middle age. That thought had gone through his head too many times already. He didn't need to compound the message.

"So you're the only one in the office today?" he ventures. "I thought I was going to be the only person here by myself all day long. I was expecting to get overrun by this big mass of customers who would all get pissed off because there's nobody here to wait on them, and then tomorrow I'd get fired for being so slow."

"The company is just saving money after the holidays. I understand them cutting hours this time of year. Most people have places to go and things to do on a holiday week, so they're glad to have the extra time off. I need the hours, so I don't mind working at all. They asked me and I told them yes."

"Nobody asked me anything. They just put me on the schedule. Guess they figure I don't have any kind of social life, so it didn't matter."

Debbie doesn't say anything, but just keeps shuffling through paid-out slips and a stack of unopened envelopes. She never looks up and doesn't bother continuing the conversation.

David asks her if she had a nice Christmas and if she was planning anything for New Year's Eve, but after a few monosyllabic half-hearted replies he can tell she'd just as soon he'd go away and have his conversation with one of the rental rug shampooers over by the Out door. He takes another good look at her bent head and the back of her neck as she goes through her paperwork and decides she's really even plainer, un-pretty, and more uninspiring than he'd originally given her credit for being, so he gives up and goes back to his post. Nothing's happening and Whitney Houston is on the satellite singing and he gets tired of standing trying to think of something to do with his hands. He folds them in front of him and joins them behind his back and sticks them in his front pockets, and it all begins to become a tiresome repetitive cycle, so he walks down to the end of the check lanes and walks back looking down each of the long aisles to see if he can spot any sign of life. He sees no one. He could hike through Death Valley at high noon and see more signs of life than this.

He's so bored he decides to amuse himself, so he begins quoting "High Flight" as if it is a mantra. Besides the lyrics to every Moody Blues song, David knows this poem by heart. He remembers learning it back in junior high, sitting at his desk and memorizing it in class while teachers talked about a bunch of shit he didn't want to know about.

"Oh! I have slipped the surly bonds of earth,
And danced the skies on laughter-silvered wings;"

He looks back at the partition and sees the top of Debbie Deason's head, but it is like she is not there, she doesn't exist. It is like he has been banished to a distant land, another planet, a place where all those involved in the business of living won't have to come across him and have him getting in the way of their progress.

"Up, up the long, delirious, burning blue
I've topped the wind-swept heights with easy grace
Where never lark or even eagle flew —"

Well, fuck this, he thinks.

Other than Whitney finding the greatest love of all and his own whispered rendition of John Gillespie Magee, Jr.'s poem, it is so quiet in the store he can hear the squeak of his Nikes on the concrete making their sound as he leaves his checkout area and walks back to the time clock just through the backroom doors. He finds his time card and positions it on the tray under the clock, pushes the lever down and hears the satisfying click that tells him his work shift for this day is through. It is not only done for this day but is done for all-time too. His Abington Home Hardware career is over. He tells himself he will go get into his van and leave the lot and worry about what he is going to do later, that this wasted portion of his life is done and he is glad. He can't take it anymore, that he knows. He'll go find something else. Hell, he thinks, the new store is probably hiring. He'd as soon be there as anywhere else.

"And, while with silent lifting mind I've trod
The high untrespassed sanctity of space,
Put out my hand, and touched the face of God."

He walks by the checkout lanes and the Customer Service desk and keeps on going out the door. He does not tell Debbie Deason he is leaving. He sees his van sitting alone in the empty lot and hears the automatic doors close behind him and walks away wondering if anyone will ever actually know he is gone, either on this day or next week or ever.

***

Five o'clock and closing time arrives. Miller, feeling like one of the survivors of Little Big Horn, considers the day a success because everyone has lived through the last-ditch retail onslaught without a death in the ranks or any other form of catastrophe. Even the borrowed cashiers have presented no problem during the day—Miller took care to relieve them for timely breaks and not talk to them like they were a part of a chain gang, and it seems to have brought out the best in them. He's pretty sure they would have rather been over here with him in the old store today than be stuck in the new one watching their bosses have nervous breakdowns and taking it all out on them.

One thing Miller knows for certain is there is no one who ever worked at Overton's that knew how to treat people and get more out of them than him. He's convinced he could take a select group of people into the new store next week and make twice the profit the current crew is going to bring in during Grand Opening. The thing is everybody already there knows it too. This is why they've been begging him for so long to move into a management position with them, so they can keep a close eye on him and try and make him fit in with them as an equal and act like they are as good at their jobs as he is, but Miller is having nothing to do with such a scenario. He knows how he likes to operate, and moving into their world would do nothing but make him miserable. He's miserable enough already. He doesn't need any help.

They lock the doors and say goodbye to the substitute cashiers and everybody's ready to go home for the day, but like all the other times in their history of working together it is like everyone is unable to simply load up in cars and trucks and ride away. Instead they find themselves leaning on John's pickup truck talking, putting the tailgate down and sitting under the stars, sharing Bud Lights from a twelve pack that John was going to take to his parents' and get the best of after stuffing himself with the supper his mother cooked for him. It is like, yes, they are older, and, yes, they have moved on from the days and nights when they were wild as two-dick dogs and wanted to drink whatever spirit they could get their hands on, and smoke all the pot and maybe delve into something with a little more kick they could come up with, and ride around all night with music blasting looking for girls knowing they would never find exactly the one they were looking for--and really, to be honest, they would give thanks to god for that because then the epic search would be over and done and what were they supposed to do tomorrow?--but it is as if now, this night, they have stepped back and revisited that part of themselves momentarily, and now they are savoring it before the time comes to move on. If only for a moment, it is nice to be like they used to be, nice to be in this hallowed stationary patch of land where such things now past once took place.

"Anybody remember Charlie Ridge?" Sammy sets his tall boy down long enough to light a cigarette. "I keep expecting that crazy old son of a bitch to show up and help us close this place down in style."

"Charlie Ridge?" Phillip smiles. "He couldn't go an hour without sneaking out to his truck for a shot of Ancient Age to keep him going. If he was around we'd all be too pickled to get anything done."

"Doesn't sound like the worst idea I've ever heard," says John.

"Well, if he shows up, be sure and let me know," says Miller. "I'll call the newspaper so they can send one of their ace reporters out, since old Charlie's been dead at least ten years now."

"God, I didn't even know he was dead," says Phillip.

"Ten years?" John asks. "Has it really been that long? Jeez."

"Longer than that, I imagine," says Miller.

"Speaking of hail, hail, the gang's all here," Sammy says, "look who's coming."

Lurching into the lot comes David in his van, the Caravan on two wheels making the entrance and speeding across the pavement, faster than David ever goes, since he generally tends to poke along like he has all day. They watch the van almost hit a bascart return rack and swerve around it, straighten up and keep barreling toward them. For a minute the question is in their minds whether this damn fool is going to actually stop or just run them down where they're gathered, but the brakes get slammed and there is a screeching sound and the van comes to a stop. The engine keeps running and the Moody Blues are blasting away. The windows are up, but everybody can hear "Go Now" loud and clear.

The driver's door opens and David's two feet emerge first, stretched out like they are testing the area for poisonous vapors, sneakered-toes sniffing the world to see if there's anything noxious lurking. Two feet descend in slow motion and balance unsteadily on the asphalt, then the rest of David follows out of the seat. He takes a step and decides that is probably enough for now and takes hold of the door handle to stand for a moment until the swaying ceases and he is halfway certain he is probably not going to fall over. None of them have ever seen this sight before, David out of his mind tottering before them, but there is no denying that he is as drunk as Pepe Le Pew on the scent of new-found amour. All he needs is a white stripe down his back and the transformation would be complete.

"Ya'll look like you're having a party," he grins.

"What in the name of god have you been up to?" Sammy asks. "You look like you've been through the car wash without the goddamned car."

"I've been celebrating," David says. "Gave myself a late Christmas present, so I thought I needed to do something to commemorate such a momentous occasion." He reaches inside the van and brings out a bottle of some form of reddish wine, twists the cap off and takes a heroic swig. They can tell he hates the taste but is being brave about it, getting done what has to get done. "I parted ways with AHH today," he announces. "Nice guy that I am, I gave them a ten second notice before I walked out the door. I imagine that right this minute the entire organization is in a frenzy, reeling over my loss, knowing they will never achieve the financial highs they experienced while I was there in their employ. But such is the case of economics in this hard world, boys. Sometimes you're at the top, then, by god and the little Lord Jesus, suddenly you drop."

Even though this is quite a spectacle and a really big show and audiences would shell out a bundle of dough to view such a sight, everybody knows this is not some extravaganza to take in without wondering what sort of risks were involved in the creation of it. David—and they all know this for certain—has never partaken of extended gulps of alcohol or anything else mind-altering to any great extent in his life so far, and now here he stands before them, unbalanced, discombobulated, altogether blind-running, hammered to his gills, so how is anyone supposed to react? What's to be thought or done? It's not like you can grin and nod and understand how a guy has to walk the tight-rope every now and then or else go crazy, because this is David, and this is crazy right here, and crazy like this is not something David has ever done and has never been expected by any of them ever to do in this lifetime. Because it's one thing to jump off the merry-go-round every now and then; it's another to wander off and go lay down on the railroad tracks and wait for the big locomotive puffing diesel smoke to come run you over.

"Wine, David?" Phillip says. "What's with that? You been having Communion in the van on the way over here?"

"Me and the Holy Spirit thought it was time for a little toast to better days."

David decides to take an exploratory amble away from the van. It goes pretty good for a few steps, then he has to stop and regroup.

"I was hoping I'd get here before you locked up," he says to Miller. "I've got to take a piss like King Kong hanging it off the Empire State Building's observation deck." He looks off toward the dark store longingly. "Oh, well, guess I'll just drive around back and cut loose. Ain't like it's never been done before."

He heads back to the van and gets in, takes off with the Moody Blues synthesizing to beat all hell and the driver's door open that he's forgotten to close. None of them standing around watching are brain surgeons or nuclear physicists, but it doesn't take much to see that just traveling the thirty or so yards around to the back of the store is not going to be that easy of a journey for old David. The Caravan shimmies and tilts a little to the left and then back to the right, and whatever potholes are in the ancient parking lot the van's tires find and embrace as its own. The headlights bounce up and down off the top of the store roof and down to the sidewalk. David is going maybe fifteen miles an hour but is driving so herky-jerky it looks like he's going seventy on Abington's bumpiest potholed road.

They stand in place holding cans of Bud Light watching the van heading its way toward the back portion of the store.

It takes about five seconds for David and the Caravan to make a direct hit with the building.

Maybe the van isn't going all that fast, but the collision is loud and impressive enough. Sammy doesn't know whether the Caravan is going to fold up like an accordion or if the building is going to cave at one point and the rest of the store follow suit like a set-up board of dominos. The sound is somewhere between a sonic boom and the apex of the O.K. Corral gunfight, and he's pretty sure it's not one of those typical evening sounds around town that is not going to draw any attention. People are going to want to know whether they are under enemy attack or the end of the world is nigh or what in the name of god is happening in their usually-peaceful hamlet of Abington.

"Aw, shit," says Miller. This is something he truly doesn't need right now.

After about a ten second countdown amid the beginning of "Knights in White Satin," David's left foot protrudes from the cab and tests the sidewalk the van has run up on for stability. He leans his body out and first surveys the building that has currently become a part of his vehicle, then swivels his neck around to see if his audience is still around watching the show he's just put on for them or if maybe they've grown bored with tonight's entertainment and headed for home. He seems pleased to see everyone is still present, so he lifts his arm and waves at them all, like he is a traveler from another world who can't quite decide if he is coming or going but might as well be friendly either way.

John is the first to walk up to the van.

"It appears to me," he says, looking over the busted headlights and crumpled metal, "you might be in the market for a new van."

"Well shit, I don't have a job anymore," David giggles. "How am I going to afford one?" The fact that he is destitute, unemployed, in the aftermath of a collision with an unmovable object, and drunker than Hooty Brown all at the same time makes him laugh again. It's been a while since he's had this much fun.

"It might not be the most kosher thing to do right now, but we need to move this van, like pronto." Phillip walks around to the front to see if the tires are flat or still inflated and how mashed the front end actually is. "It wouldn't do for it to be sitting like this when the cops get here."

Like a cue from a stagehand, the sound of a siren becomes audible down the road, grows a little louder and nearer each second they listen to it.

"No, don't move it," Miller says. "Leave it right where it is." He walks over to the driver's side and looks at David. "Can you walk, or do I need to go inside and get a fucking two-wheeler to move your ass? You need to be away from this van before the cops get here. You need to be over there with everybody else acting like an innocent bystander. And, everybody, we need to get rid of the beer. Throw it in the dumpster. We don't need them to see it and start thinking we're having a party out here."

"If this is a party, I'm leaving right now," says Sammy. "There's got to be better festivities than this going on somewhere."

"What we're doing, guys, is we're in the process of staging an accident." Miller walks around the van, pointing here and there like a professor giving a lecture, providing his students hints about just what might be on the upcoming test. "We were all just standing here in the lot talking, see, and David got out of his van and forgot to put it in Park, and so it rolled off and hit the building. Just an accident, that's what it was. No harm, no foul. The store isn't really damaged at all—just the van—and even if the building actually happens to be fucked up it's getting ready to be torn down next week anyway, so there's no reason to make a big deal out of it."

"Here," Sammy says to David. "Give me your wallet." He takes David's wallet and hands his back to David. "For the next few minutes I'm you and you're me, get it? I'm David the dumbass owner of the van, and you're Sammy, the cool and handsome owner of the Corvette parked over there. Just keep your trap closed and don't even think about touching my goddamn car."

A police cruiser pulls up beside them and idles for a moment, looking them over to see if any Manson Family members might be present, checking out the van intermingling with the store, wondering if the New Year's craziness is starting early and this is going to be one of those holiday seasons to remember here in Abington.

"Had an accident, gentlemen?" the first officer asks. He and his partner are both out of the cruiser now and strolling around checking for signs of shiftiness, reckless endangerment, perhaps a prior felony or two hidden in the haystack somewhere.

"I was talking to my friends," Sammy says, "and after a minute or two I got out of the van and accidentally left the damn thing in Drive. It took off and I couldn't stop it—rolled right over there and plowed into the store." He smiles at the officers like he is someone you'd like as a brother-in-law. "I'm used to doing stupid shit sometimes, but this one sort of takes the cake."

"It looks like you messed up your car pretty good," says the cruiser's driver. He shines his flashlight on the front of the van and whistles. "I'm not so sure that's something that can be fixed or not." He looks at the building and turns around and speaks to Miller. "Don't you work here?" he asks.

"We all do," says Miller. "We just closed up for the day."

"I thought I knew you. I come in here a lot in the mornings. I hear they're fixing to close this place down. Is that right?"

"Last day's Saturday." Miller points off in the distance. "The new store's over there. It opens next week."

"The building doesn't look like it's hurt," the first cop says to Sammy. "We could fill out a report for insurance purposes, I guess, but it's one of those private property no-fault type of things, so I guess you can just deal with it with your insurance company the best way you can. Since the building's coming down

soon anyway I don't guess it matters all that much."
He looks at Sammy like he's maybe forgetting
something, like maybe it might be a better idea to run
somebody in for just existing and taking up space, but
then he changes his mind. "You do have insurance,
don't you?"

"Yes, sir." Sammy whips out David's billfold and
starts thumbing through it like he knows what he's
doing and is so on top of it all. "I've got my card right
here."

"We don't need it. Just call them yourself and get it
taken care of that way." He turns to Miller. "You're
the boss here, right?"

"I'm in charge until this coming Saturday," Miller
says. "All the really big bosses have already moved
over to the new store."

"Then I'll let you handle it. I don't see a whole lot
of sense in doing a bunch of paperwork over
something that's going to be gone this time next week.
We'll just let it ride for tonight. You fellows have a
good evening." He turns to Sammy and points at the
van. "Good luck fixing your van."

"I imagine," Sammy smiles, "it's pretty much done
for. I've been thinking of buying a new one anyway."

The cops drive off and everybody stands in a circle
looking at each other, all of them more than shocked
with how easily this has all gone down. Sammy walks
over to David and hands him his wallet back, keeps his
palm outstretched until he gets his own back. "This
wasn't much of a trade," he says. "I checked to see
how much money you had and you were even more
broke than me. That's pretty damn bad in my book."

"I've got a paycheck coming from AHH tomorrow," David remembers. "I'll have to go back in to get it. God, I'll hate doing that."

"You could donate it as a way of making up for screwing them over today, walking out and stuff," says John. "I'll bet AHH would be happy to get a little reimbursement to get them through the shock and trauma of losing their number one employee."

"Maybe you can get your job back if you tell them how sorry you are for what you did," says Phillip.

"Shit, I'm not sorry. I should have walked out a long time ago. I never should have gone to work there to begin with."

David is tired of talking about it. He wanders over to look at what used to be his van. He'd left the bottle of wine on the passenger seat, and he wonders how either of the two cops managed not to see it sitting there. The answer is because they are inept, sorry excuses for police officers, piss-poor at what they are paid to do, just like everybody else in this town, himself included. Especially him. He decides from here on out he's going to have to do better. He's going to have to figure some of this shit out.

He unscrews the cap and chugs some more wine down, almost finishing it off. What's left he does not want anymore, so he lays it back in the van. He looks over at a dumpster around the back of the store. It looks like as good a place as any to go barf.

***

Miller gets everyone organized pushing David's van off the sidewalk and away from the back wall of the store. He doesn't think it really matters that much, but he leaves the van in Drive and attempts to move it to the far end of the parking lot for the night to let it sit there until he can get it towed off tomorrow morning. He could just leave it and call Jim and let him know what's going on, but fuck that, he doesn't want to talk to Laurel's better half right now. He doesn't want anybody at the new store coming over to screw with what's going on in his territory. There may just be two days left to go now, but he doesn't need anybody coming by to tell him what to do with this building they really don't want anything to do with anymore. Let them stay over in the promised land. He'll stay here. It will work out better that way.

The hell of it is the van won't for some strange reason wish to go forward in Drive, so Sammy jams it back into Neutral and they push the hulk of fractured metal as far back toward the back property line as possible. When Miller tries to take the keys out of the ignition he can't get them to come out. He tries to slam the lever back into Park but it's no deal. He can't turn the engine off and he can't get the keys out, so he has to leave it running.

"Hey," he says to David, "looks like you're fucked."

"What else is new?" David says. "Don't worry about it. Leave it. I'm sick of worrying about it. It's a wrecked van. How important can it be?"

"How are you going to get in your apartment? I can't get the rest of your keys off the ring." Phillip says. "You got another key?"

"I'll break a window. I'll sleep out in the parking lot. I'll call the apartment manager. Hell, I'll go home with you and sleep with Janet," he says. All at once he feels good and free. "You can sleep by yourself out on the living room couch." "That's maybe a pretty good idea," says Phillip. "It's about time I did something to make her happy."

FRIDAY, DECEMBER 30

David can't help but notice how everybody here inside his former place of employment at AHH walks right by him and acts like they don't know who he is this morning. He is not really sure if this is because they all know about how he just walked off and quit without notice yesterday or if it is simply an extension of how it has always been since the first week of his employment, when it started dawning on his associates that he was not truly one of them and undoubtedly never was going to be.

Whatever the case, it still feels pretty awkward standing in line behind a customer at the front desk waiting to get his paycheck. It's not so much that he is ashamed of himself for walking out yesterday—hell, these folks almost deserved it for the way they'd treated him the past couple of years, acting like he was some stupid scum of the earth type—but he doesn't relish asking for his check like they are doing him a favor to hand it over to him, or even worse, having to answer anyone's question about why he did what he did on Thursday. In a perfect world he wouldn't be in a situation like this. In a perfect world, damn it, he would have never been around here in the first place. He would be teaching an art class or working in commercial art somewhere or doing something the tiniest bit satisfying. He would have never gone and married two women—one a religious nut who decided he might be possessed by evil spirits and so divorced him, the other a moron who loved prescription drugs and figured he ought to work two or three jobs all the time to buy them for her—and he would have never started worrying about status and money and all that kind of crap, acting like a damn fool for almost ten years. He would have just stayed at Overton's and come home in the evening and stayed in his room. He could have spent his time drawing and sketching and playing his guitar and reading comic books and that would have been just fine. As it was, he'd had to stop doing a lot of things that made him happy and entered into some shitty existences where everything around him sucked the majority of the time.

And he included himself at the head of the pack of all those things that sucked. He was nothing but a fuckup.

But no more.

Nobody gives him any flak about Thursday, which is good. He just gets his check and gets told to have a nice day and he's out the door with the worst of his imagined plight behind him. He's borrowed John's truck to come over here and now drives back to the store to take it back and then decide what to do with the wrecked Caravan. In the light of day, it doesn't look like there's all that much of a decision to be made. The van looks like toast to him. He'll have to turn it over to insurance and see what happens and how soon he can get something else, but right now it's just not in his resolve to worry over anything that requires money to operate, because money is presently not something he has a lot of. He's just happy both his parents are out at the cemetery and not around to see him fuck up like this. He would have had a hell of a time explaining everything to them.

"Hell," John tells him, "if it's bothering you that much about your van, don't get anything right now. If you're not planning on going to Florida or migrating to Canada any time soon, then you're more than welcome to go over to my parents' house and get my old bike out of the garage. I saw it yesterday. Wipe the twenty years' worth of cobwebs off and put some air in the tires and you'll be all set. It'll do you good to pedal around a while. You can get rid of all that whale blubber you've been accumulating eating your weight in TV dinners every time you sit down at a table."

"Since I'm a professional wino now I can concentrate on drinking every night and not have to worry about getting pulled over on the way home. I'll be DUI-proof and worry-free riding a bike. I'm beginning to like this idea already."

"Then there you go," says John.

"Now all I have to do is find a job somewhere."

"There's the new store right over there." John motions with his thumb. "You did your thing at this store for a while, you can go do it over there too. I'm sure you're qualified to do something."

"I'm a hell of a bagger," David says. "I think the future is starting to reveal itself to me."

"Man, I should be so lucky," says John.

***

By mid-morning the traffic in the store has come to a halt. Miller, knowing they have put this off for about as long as they can, calls Sammy to the front and says it's past time for the two of them to go over to the new store and get their training in on the new system, ordering and checking and such.

"Like I don't know how to do any of it," says Sammy.

"Like neither of us do," says Miller, "but we have to go sometime. Deanna's been calling over here all week bugging the shit out of me about it. I think they're afraid they're going to open next week and you and me won't know the first thing to do." "We can stick our fingers up our asses. We're both damn good at that." "We do enough of that already."

They walk over, despite the fact there's a northwest wind whistling through the empty lot between the buildings trying to go right through them. Sammy, in his shirtsleeves, doesn't seem to notice, jacket or a coat being one of those items he has always considered unnecessary baggage. Miller, however, is freezing his ass off. He knows he's getting older by the way he can't stand the cold anymore. The least little chill and he starts turning blue.

"I even hate the way this damn place looks from the outside." Sammy drags on a Marlboro and nods his head at the new building. "I already know I'm going to hate it when I get inside even more than I do now. That's the main reason I haven't been over to check it out much. I can't stand the idea of being in there trapped and surrounded by a bunch of bullshit fifty hours a week."

The new Overton's is bright and clean and modern, everything the old store is not and hasn't been close to being anytime in the recent past. There are twice as many checkout lanes, enhanced signing and wide aisles. There is a deli and a bakery, a floral shop and a video rental store. Hot foods are available inside a compact restaurant, and pizzas are prepared for takeout in a cheese shop. There are rumors about a bank moving in soon along with a pharmacy. It is like a small city set down in the center of Abington, and Miller wonders when beds will be added to the mix so customers can spend the night if they get tired doing their shopping and need to rest up a little.

Miller sees Deanna and Laurel in the office, their backs to them looking at something on a computer screen, like something that's going on in a store that hasn't even opened yet is the most important thing in the world. Here I go, he thinks. I can tell already this is not going to be pretty.

Jim unlocks the front door and lets them in. He is anxious to show both of them around the aisles so they can see how well-stocked and orderly everything is, maybe insinuating to Sammy and Miller in one way or another what a good job he and his staff are doing over here without the two of them being in the mix. Sammy sees all the workers and vendors putting stock up and thinks how he has never seen as many people as this working in the old store the entire time he's been there. And yes, he knows, as soon as everything's in place and the opening is done with all this excess help will disappear and it will be him and Miller left behind in the trenches once again trying to keep the place from sinking like the Bismarck to the bottom of the Grocery Sea.

Sammy and Miller walk the aisles listening to Jim expound on what a fabulous job he's been doing and how wonderful everything is going to be from here on out. Everything they get shown they've seen already, everything being basically the same as the old store other than the fact that it's new and modern and has additional buttons to push and steps to take, so with all that most of their training is pretty much done in five minutes.

"I don't really think there's all that much more to do other than keep stocking and getting these shelves filled up," Jim says. "I think you guys can get over here Tuesday or so and get oriented on everything else in one day. It's not like you don't both know anything about how to run a grocery store. One day will be more than enough for you." One day will be more than enough to make me want to burn the goddamned place down, thinks Sammy.

I wonder if this dumbass Jim has any idea how long I've been screwing his wife, Miller thinks.

The grand tour completed, they walk up to the front office to check it out and to say hello to Deanna and Laurel. There are camera monitors and a money order machine and a screen to pay utility bills, cartons of cigarettes and file cabinets and letter trays for everyone's mail and store reports. Miller looks it over and looks at Laurel's leg where she's sitting in her chair by an accounting table with a bill counter and piles of money bands stacked up neatly in rows. When Sammy goes with Deanna and Jim to take a look at the receiving dock Miller and Laurel are left alone, looking out through the plexiglass at people skittering to and fro, like all their asses are on fire from some imaginary flame and there's no fire department anywhere to come and put it out.

"You've been among the missing again. I haven't heard from you," Laurel says. She looks at him with her Pacific-blue eyes, like she wants him to gaze deeply within them and tell her everything he never has before. He doesn't have to waste any words telling her how that's not very close to happening right this moment.

"Busy times for everyone," he tells her. "I didn't want to come in here and I didn't want to call, too many eyes and ears around, and I never knew when you were at home or at work."

"I don't think that's the real reason."

"You're probably right. It might be there's just not that much for us to talk about right now. Conversations don't seem to be getting us anywhere lately."

"I've got something to tell you that you really need to know."

"Really? Because I thought I was pretty much up to date on everything."

"I haven't been feeling very good for a few days, Miller. I missed my period." She turns her eyes on him to make sure he gets this all down. "I waited a couple of days and then bought one of those pregnancy kits. I don't have to paint you a picture of what it said."

"That is interesting. I guess the question has to arise as to whether it's mine or not? The next question is how come the pill didn't work?"

"I wondered if that was the road you were going to go down. Answer one, I don't know if it's yours or not. And answer number two is I stopped taking the pill because it kept making me feel bad."

"Yeah, well, you know I've wondered for a long time now if something like this was going to happen. You tell me you and Jim aren't together much, so maybe I'm supposed to assume that I'm the lucky papa. But there's always been something that tells me you now and then burn the candle on both ends sometimes. You say you want to be with me but then you seem to want to stay where you are too. I don't ever get this cozy feeling that when the final choice gets made and it's all said and done that I'm going to be the guy in the winner's circle holding your hand for the photographers to shoot color pictures for the society page. See, Laurel, I think you decided to marry into some Overton money to save yourself from a lot of bad shit you were into before you came to Abington, and then somewhere along the way the money started not meaning that much to you anymore, and there I was, Johnny on the spot again. I was good to get you through some empty cold nights and make you feel better, but I don't really think you ever thought it very damn likely you and me were going to wind up together for good."

"I think about you and me all the time, Miller. I don't really know what you mean when you say things like that. What I know is you have never told me anything about how you were feeling about you and me being together one way or the other. I never have known what you're thinking, so it's hard for me on my own to make any kind of plan. I'm beginning to wonder what's going to become of us if things keep up this way," she says, like she's in a movie and everybody needs to stop crunching popcorn and listen up and take note.Miller doesn't answer. Silence seems a good option, since it's not every day he gets confronted with the idea that he may or may not be a father pretty soon, so a period of thought and contemplation may be in order before any form of negotiation begins to take shape.

Sometimes, he thinks, the hits just keep on coming.

Sammy, having seen enough of the new Overton's now to make him want to skip lunch to keep from throwing it up and tired of nodding his head agreeing with all the starry talk he's been hearing, is back up front and outside the office door, so Miller zips his coat and opens the door and walks out without further discussion about what exactly is going wrong and amiss with his and Laurel's relationship. Brother, he thinks, why don't I go home and write *War and Peace* and explain every little twist and turn about it to all the folks in the world who are interested. Right now, though, he can't think of too many who'd line up to get a signed copy.

"You know, I've heard a lot of far-out crap in my life, but I think I've finally run across one that takes the goddamn cake." Sammy walks along and fishes a cigarette from his shirt, lights it up with his Bic and blows out a whirlwind of smoke in disgust. "We get back there on the dock and our esteemed boss Jim gets me off from Deanna and proceeds to tell me how he knows there's something going on between Laurel and me. He's been more than aware of it for a long time now and he wants it stopped right now."

Miller twists his head and looks up at Sammy to see if he's kidding. He can tell he's not.

"Do what?" he says

"The stupid son of a bitch thinks I'm the one hunkering down with Laurel, like he's fucking Sherlock Holmes and he's solved the big mystery because he's so goddamned wise. Damn, Miller, I was so surprised at how dumb the son of a bitch actually is that I didn't know how to answer. I just looked at him like he was crazy as hell and he just kept nodding his head like he'd won the jackpot on a game show or something. I've got to give him credit for being the most ignorant asshole who ever walked around on the planet. I've been underestimating him all this time."

Miller doesn't think there's too much that's funny about Jim's intellect, but he laughs anyway.

"I guess this means I'm in the clear," he says. "I guess from here on out I can go do anything I want, because you're the one who's going to get plugged by the jealous husband." He looks over at Sammy and shakes his head. "I'm going to miss you, Samuel. I've enjoyed working with you all these years. Overton's will never be the same without you. I'll be sure and say some kind words at your wake."

"After Saturday Overton's isn't going to ever be the damn same anyway. Me taking a goddamn bullet and dying quick might be the easiest way out. Hell, I might just like it. It might keep me from suffering too much later on. The thing of it is, though, is I just hate to die for something I didn't do. I'd at least like to be guilty of what I'm getting murdered for."

"You're guilty of plenty, don't worry about that," Miller says. "If it wasn't this it would be something else."

***

Business is so slow Miller has gone ahead and sent the two substitute cashiers back to the new store for further training and stocking help. He doesn't need them. He's got Sammy and himself here, which is really enough, and John's shown up this morning too. Phillip came in right after nine and David is going to be back after lunch. David wants a job at the new store; Miller has to see about making that happen. He meant to say something to Jim when he was over there earlier, but he had other things on his mind. Laurel, he thinks. What in god's name is he going to do about Laurel?

(When it started I didn't think a whole lot about it. I was like Sammy and it was just this big game I decided I might as well play because I wasn't doing anything else. I didn't ever believe anything would come of it and never would have done anything to further it along if it hadn't been that part of me that looked at her and thought how if I didn't do anything about it like it was

*obvious to everybody that she wanted me to they would
see right through me and know I was all show and no
go and I wasn't anything like what I appeared to be
but just wanted everybody to think I was and so I had
to go through with it and act like everybody else you
know be a goddamn All American guy go to bed with
her even if that wasn't what I really wanted because
this was the real world out here now pal and this is
how you do it that's just the way it is and all that movie
romantic book stuff you've got stitched in your head
from college and walking around in real life doesn't
exist and you ought to know that by now you ought to
know that it's never going to be that way and if you
wait on something like that to come to you something
out of a cloud a fantasy a starry dream it will never
come and there you'll be with nothing if you don't go
ahead and take what comes to you whether you like it
or not whether you've dreamed about something else
and told yourself how some day it was going to come
and then you kept seeing how it hadn't come and
wasn't coming and you wondered how you were going
to make it through how you were going to go on
forever knowing it was never going to come and you
would always forever be there with nothing.)*

It had been so long now he could not remember
when it all began. It had gone on for so long he could
not imagine it not being there. It was a hell of a thing,
all right, it was like something he read about or heard
about and shook his head at the stupid situations
people got themselves into, but he had never imagined
it would be him.

The displays have gotten so low now that it's easy
to look out the front window and see the traffic out on
Clement Drive, and Miller sees a tow truck pulling
David's van out of the lot, on the way, he'd wager, to

the automobile elephant graveyard. David walks behind it pushing a bicycle up the walk, his head studying the concrete, purposely not watching his faithful old Dodge Caravan disappear from the scene. Miller wonders what is going through David's mind right now, what, exactly, his crazy friend thinks of being jobless and auto-less and nursing an unfamiliar hangover all in the space of one funny night. For a little he would feel sorry for him, but then he considers the way David has acted the last few years, angry, moody, unfeeling, aloof, sometimes rejecting his friends and going through two divorces on top of it all, and maybe, Miller thinks, something like this little shit pie lesson needs to come along for him to help him learn how to put an end to it. Maybe old David just needs to hit rock bottom with a resounding thud, take himself an eight count, and then see how the rest of the match goes on from there. Perhaps this is a wake-up call. Tough going, Miller is sure, and he hates to have no pity about it, but that's the way it goes for everybody sometimes. Who knows, maybe he is fixing to go to a similar version of Hell on earth himself.

Phillip can hardly take all this standing around much longer. He likes it better when everything is hectic and fast-paced and he doesn't have time to think, because he's learned from the past that too much meditation and reflection are the things that tend to get him in trouble the most. He comes out from behind his register and takes a seat on the end of the check lane. He looks out the front window and watches the traffic go back and forth and sees how the sky is Russian novel gray and the world is one big cloud holding the coming of winter over the city's head. He wonders if the New Year will bring in a blanket of snow. School will start back on Tuesday, but if there's snow then classes will be canceled and the holiday break will go on. At this moment he doesn't know if he wants to stay on Christmas break or return to real life.

"The more I think about it," John says, fishing a cigarette out of his pack, "the more I'm inclined to not go back to McGinnis next week. I've been thinking about it a lot. It's not like working with McGinnis Electric is the only job in the world, and it's not like living up there in God's country is anything to write home about."

"Plenty of jobs here, I suppose." Phillip thinks to hell with it and lights a cigarette too without getting up and going outside. No one is around to complain about him smoking on the front end and he doubts if the floor is going to ever get swept again anyway. "I don't know if the pay is as good here as what you're getting there, but you'd at least be home again. You'd at least be back on familiar turf."

"Sometimes this feels like home, but then sometimes it doesn't. Sometimes, when I come back to Abington, I turn a corner and I don't know where the hell I am anymore."

"Everything changes, buddy. Nothing stays the same, whether it still physically looks like it always did or not."

The afternoon drags on, and the consensus is whatever business is going to come before the doors close for good is going to be on Saturday, New Year's Eve. It is like the bargain hunters of Abington have made a final retreat to regroup, and so now there is not much to do but sit and smoke and watch the day draw to a close, everybody feeling like they are joined together here in some sort of Alamo, knowing there is one final onslaught to come before it is over and done and wondering if they will make it through alive and unscathed or be forced to go down swinging.

Miller closes down fifteen minutes early because it is so slow, and the group meeting in the parking lot after the doors are locked is not so prolonged and sociable as usual, not like it has been earlier in the week between the old friends and compatriots of this old store. It is almost like everyone has decided to follow suit with the shoppers, to take a deep breath and garner some solitude and mete out some resolve and gather themselves before the final day begins. All this is not spoken by anyone and no one wants anyone else to see the level of seriousness that has fallen upon them, but it is best to go to separate corners now and find some form of balm in the ticking of a clock and the passage of time. Sammy gets in his Vette and blasts off out of the lot, the deep-throated muffler noise roaring and the tires peeling rubber above the Abington traffic out on Clement. David rides around in a circle on the English Racer, attempting to do a wheelie and failing, wondering if he can possibly pedal two miles to his apartment without suffering a stroke. John and Phillip load up in John's truck, driving down the road toward home with John punching the buttons on the car radio like a jukebox, trying with each jab to find a song he really wants to hear.

No luck so far.

Phillip gets out at his in-law's house and John drives away up to the four-way stop, where he sits for a moment with the engine idling and the radio turned off because all he can seem to find to listen to is either George Michael telling him to have faith or Bobby McFerrin advising him to not worry and be happy. Such philosophical consultations he does not desire right now, and the silence inside the cab of the truck is thick with the grinding of his mind. The screeching and groaning between his ears is unsettling, and he knows going back to sit and chat with his parents that this evening is not going to cut it as far as keeping some semblance of peace in his life for these last few hours of 1988.

Luckily, he remembers that this is Friday night, and on Friday night his parents like to go out with their friends and eat fish at Red Lobster. He is thankful he can go home to some peace and not have to answer questions or tell dutiful lies, but he thinks how there will be nothing there for him to eat unless he decides to prepare it himself, and that is not going to happen. He does enough of that in blessed McGinnis after long days at work, comes home and fixes supper and falls asleep in the recliner with the TV on some sporting event, does it with some degree of regularity when he doesn't opt for going out to some tavern or bar to drink his dinner from a bottle or a frosted mug. He wonders if there is somewhere in Abington he can go and get a quick bite before the demons and hobgoblins overrun his senses and get the best of him one more time.

He's not really fooling himself, and he admits it inside his head when he finds himself in his old driveway looking at his old house, trying to decide if it is uninhabited at the moment or if signs of life exist within. He feels pretty damn stupid sitting here, if the truth is known, closer to being a total creep than he ever thought he'd be, but the fact is he is sitting here anyway in his ex-wife Carol's driveway that once used to be half-his thinking how if anybody passes by they will assume he is here to kill her and call the police to stop this possibly tragic domestic disturbance from happening. He knows it is nothing like that and would like to explain it to Carol if it is possible, but it is

Friday night and she is probably not at home, she may be out on a date with some guy who might be a cut above him when it comes down to it, or she may even be inside the house looking out the curtains and dialing the police at this very time, telling them to hurry and get here, hurry up, please, because my ex-husband is outside, and he may be crazy, and I think it could be he's dropped by on his way home this Friday night to murder me perhaps.

While he's wondering if he should go find a phone booth and give her a call, the side door to the kitchen opens and Carol peeks out and spots him sitting in the truck. She's either brave as hell or has decided from profound curiosity to see what he wants, because she comes out the door and walks toward him. It is hard for John to decide if she is glad to see him and, like him, wants to talk, or if she's packing a handgun on her and is just getting close enough and in range to blow his brains out and be done with it. In a quick flash it comes to him how he has never been able to determine exactly where Carol is coming from at any particular time, but then he supposes she could make the same statement about him. It's not like there have ever been too many moments of clarity between them, when they were both on the same page at the same time.

It's getting colder than a witch's tit, so he reaches over and opens the passenger door, knowing he'll be a better target that way if that's the way it's going to be. What the hell, he thinks.

"I was wondering if you were just turning around, or if you were here for a reason." Carol examines the truck's interior for a moment, the crumpled cardboard cups in the floor, a Burger King Whopper container, the ashtray overflowing with butts, then decides she's seen worse and slides in. "I take it there's a reason for this visit," she says, "or maybe you're just dropping by to bring that late Christmas present I didn't get from Santa."

"I was on the way home from working and decided to take the long scenic route," he says. "So here I am."

"Somebody told me you were working over at Overton's. Haven't you guys got that place closed down yet?"

"One more day. Tomorrow is it."

They look at each other for a minute without speaking. They've been divorced two years, and the silence between them now is vaguely reminiscent of the old days. It is like they have both stepped back into a script which they have practiced so many times it is impossible to forget where to stand and what not to say.

"I hope I didn't freak you out the other night," John begins, "coming up to you like that out of the blue. I shouldn't have done that. I was already up there before I thought better of it. I'm sorry if it caused trouble."

"It was no trouble," Carol smiles. "It really wasn't. It was a first date that somebody at work set me up with, and it wasn't going very good. We'd been to a movie and had hardly said a word to each other the whole night. It was pretty terrible. At least when you showed up we had something to talk about later. It turned out he had a weird ex-wife too."

"Are you saying I'm weird?"

"You're not normal, that's for sure."

"Normal is boring," he tells her, grinning. "You were never boring," she says, grinning back. John decides Carol is not going to shoot him or call the police or do both, so with all the worst-case possibilities out of the way he goes ahead and says what he's been telling himself for a long time he was never going to say.

"I'm thinking about moving back," he says. "I don't like what I'm doing and I can't stand McGinnis anymore. I don't want you to put out a contract on me, though, if I do decide to come back. I just thought I ought to let you know before I do it, give you some kind of a warning that I'm back in town again."

"You can do what you want. I don't have any claims on you."

"Maybe you do. It's not like I go days at a time not thinking about you."

She doesn't have anything to say about this, at least not yet, not out loud here in the cab of the truck. For a couple of seconds they listen to the engine idle. The white smoke from the exhaust drifts from the back of the bed up to the windshield, blending in with the night and making the few lights that are turned on in the house look like fireflies out in the country, far from the city's illumination. It's been a while since they have been together like this, just sitting and being quiet and letting all things be.

"Well," she says.

"Have you eaten anything yet?" he asks. It's like a what-the-hell question. "We could go out somewhere."

She looks at him and laughs.

"We get divorced and I sit around doing nothing for two years. I finally go out with somebody, and wouldn't you know it, you pop up," she says. She laughs again. "I'm damned if I do and damned if I don't. It's always the same with you." She laughs again. "Let me go get my purse."

***

His in-laws and his wife and daughter are sitting at the table eating dinner without him when he comes in, so Phillip goes into the guest bedroom and dumps his keys and billfold and changes his shirt. It occurs to him how far he must have tumbled off the high priority list for the family as of this moment, since dinner has begun without him even being present. It is almost as if no one actually expected him to come home from the store after closing, expected instead for him to go out again with his old friends, so why should they wait and let everything get cold? He guesses this might be a good indication that he is bordering on finding his name on the permanent shit list.

"How's everyone?" he asks. He sits down between Janet and his daughter, kisses them both on the cheek, then scoots his chair up and unfolds his napkin and places it in his lap. "Everything looks good," he says.

"So, are you folks getting the place closed down?" Janet's father asks after a few seconds of mutual chewing. Phillip is glad for the silence to be interrupted.

"All we have to do is lock the doors at five tomorrow. Other than that there's not that much else to do. There's not too much left on the shelves to buy, that's for sure." He notices how he sounds like a regular blabbermouth. "Everything's sold out for the most part.""I don't even see why you're even going in," Janet says. "If there's nothing to do, then why bother? It's not like you really need the money or anything. You should just relax and enjoy the rest of your Christmas break."

"I guess it's simply for old time's sake," he says, explaining even though he knows no one will understand what he means, which is all right, which is just in keeping with everything these days. Whatever he does, he can't explain why he does it. Whatever he doesn't do, he can't explain that either. "All us guys started out there together back in the days of yore, and it just seems like the proper thing to do is we end it together too. It's like going down with the ship." He smiles at everyone around the table, laying it out for them as best he can. He knows it's like everything else; they'll either get it or not, but he'll say it anyway and let it go at that. At least this way it won't be all inside him with him being the only one who knows it. "All for one and one for all—you know what I mean?" he says. "It may be the last time we're all together. The next time around one of us might be gone for good."

He doesn't mention how he thinks that someone is probably going to be him.

Everyone nods their head and chews their food some more, keeps on eating and acting like they know what in the name of God he's talking about.

***

For Miller, it is out of the question to go through a fast food window. He's been burned too many times doing that before and something is never right. He either gets the wrong order or incorrect change or can't understand what's being said to him or the person inside can't decipher what he says to them. It's one of those things not worth the effort or the anger and frustration it brings on, so he has learned the only way to combat it is to park outside and go in, then either order to go or find a table and eat on the premises. He sits at a table by the window overlooking Clement and

Main, watching what is left of the rush hour make its way home past the closed-up businesses and used car lots and the festering pawn shops that seem to lately be multiplying, people going broke and having to sell all their prized possessions just so they can survive another week or two. He can remember when such a non-southern evil as a pawn shop never existed in the town of Abington. Pawn shops were too urban and belonged too much to some cinema version of New York City and the big cities to the north and east, but now there are three of them in a row on Main Street, all in competition with each other. It is another one of those things about his hometown that is not what he conjectures when the name Abington comes up.

He looks at the cheeseburger on the open wrapper before him and notices how it is not the same either. It sits before him ready to be eaten, but he cannot help looking at it and seeing how the bun seems not so brown, the meat not so familiar, not so much in the category of being defined as mystery but just not so juicy and promising as he remembered a cheeseburger once to be. He imagines how he can take bites of it and consume it and be sated as far as hunger goes, but during the act of chewing and swallowing something will be missing. Without taking the first bite he knows already his meal will be nothing to write home about. It will be like everything on the menu, here, everywhere in town he bothers to go, fair to middling, average, only a cut above mediocre. If he had any energy he would take the time to shop and eat at home, but he is a sitting duck there; he is either alone and waiting to hear more breaking news from Laurel, or he is out of his mind on something and trying to keep himself from going out into the night and allowing all sorts of trouble to find him.

It's Friday night, the next to last night of the year, and tomorrow is Saturday, New Year's Eve, and tomorrow, he tells himself, is it. Overton's is kaput when the bell tolls five. Or, he amends, Overton's as he knows it. This building he's looked at today is something foreign to his sight, something he hasn't brought himself to consider as being viable and real just yet. It is getting late, though. He wonders when he is going to broach the subject in his head.

He doesn't have to be alone right now. He could actually be with Laurel if he'd made any kind of an effort to do so. He'd locked the doors and drove past the new store and seen Jim's car parked there and Laurel's car gone, and he knew she was home waiting for him to call so she could know whether to come to his house or not. But he hadn't called. Instead he'd come inside this franchise to eat an imitation cheeseburger, chew on some rubber fries, sip a fake milkshake, and take another long look at a town he had no idea where it had sprung up from, a town called home of which he is becoming more each day a stranger.

He doesn't want to be sitting here and he doesn't want to go home. There is some place he feels he should be, but it hasn't come to him yet.

It is becoming Friday night and it is early. He will sit and wait until the answer comes to him, although the possibility exists it may take a while.

***

Even with the parking lot lights on, it is still darker than his soul back on the dock behind the store. Sammy has parked the Vette in between a salvage trailer and a dumpster, so even if somebody like a zealous cop happens to pass by they won't see it, and he will be able to keep sitting back here in the darkness pretty much ripped out of his gourd and go undisturbed, which is exactly the way he wants it.

To hell with the world right now.

He'd fallen into a bad-ass mood this afternoon after visiting the new store and getting accused of screwing Laurel Overton, which was stupid as shit, since anybody in their right mind knows it is Laurel and Miller who are doing all the screwing and have been for years. He doesn't know who is to blame the most— Jim for being stupid, Laurel for marrying Jim for his money but still wanting to keep messing around with Miller like there is some kind of future for them someday, or Miller for letting himself get trapped in that kind of relationship with Laurel for practically goddamn forever when there are available women all over the place and it doesn't matter if they are married or not. Hell, Sammy has been telling Miller for years to get away from this thing with Laurel, she was bad news and there was never going to be anything that came from it, nothing but trouble anyway, and now here he is being blamed for being the one doing it all the while. Well, shit fire and save matches, is all he can think.

He absolutely does not know how this move from the old Overton's to the new one is going to work out. The more he looks at it the more he simply can't see himself in the new store. He looks around, his eyes accustomed to the dark now, his senses heightened to no end, at the discarded items left back in the dock well to disintegrate and rot, a work glove, a stack of rotten soda shells, somebody's rusted jump stamp from god knows when. Bascarts that won't roll or have missing wheels line the side of the building over by a ladder that goes up to the roof.

Sammy looks at the ladder.

He hadn't planned to be back on store property tonight. It is not only dark and somewhat depressing sitting here thinking of how next week at this time he won't be able to do this, but it is damn cold out here too. And for once he regrets leaving home without a jacket. He doesn't think it is going to snow or do anything drastically wintery like that, but a fellow could freeze his ass off just sitting here like this.

Especially if the fellow is stoned out of his tree by a killer joint he's smoked, which is him to a tee right now. Here he is, sitting on the dock of a dead store, not anywhere near any kind of Otis Redding moment whatsoever, no ocean waves lapping at his feet, just darkness and junk and crap and wind from the north going through him even worse than if he'd been in the Corvette with the top down on the road to who knows where. But that hadn't done it for him tonight. He'd tried riding around for a while looking for somewhere to go, then had given up and come back to the store.

The next thing he knows he's climbing the ladder to the roof like he is acquainted with old Jacob personally, and when he gets to the top he grabs the railing and pulls himself up and stands there looking at the neighborhood. Off to his left he can see the new store with the lights all blazing like Times Square and four or five cars parked in the lot, and he knows there are people, true dumbasses, in there still on this Friday night doing a bunch of shit that won't mean a thing by this time tomorrow. Straight ahead is Clement Road, the traffic all but absent now that it is Friday and the work week for normal people is done. I am not normal, Sammy grins, lighting a cigarette despite the northerly gale up here high on the rooftop, high like he is, guilty of everything and more, blowing the smoke out under the clear stars and watching it fly away, wanting to go with it, to be somewhere else, but afraid to let go, afraid he might get blown from this rooftop and land in some place where he doesn't know where everything is, where it goes and where it comes from, only that he is no longer the fellow no one can tell anything to, because he is now just another one of those guys who once knew it all.

To his right is the old neighborhood, his house, his high school, the places where his friends lived, churches, stores, graveyards. It has been a while since he has looked down upon them; he has not climbed up here in a long time. The view is different now. A lot of things are gone.

(*When we had new* employees *I used to like to mess with them. I'd send them back to the stock room to get a skyhook, tell them to go to Aisle Four and bring back a twenty-five-pound bag of prunes, and at night send them up this very ladder here to sweep the roof. We'd stand outside laughing our asses off hearing that broom going back and forth*).

Just that moment it comes to him that he is not so altogether stoned right now. It is a false high he has and he knows it. His senses are not heightened and there is nothing new forming in his mind. He is the same old guy. He is not up here for any exhilarating epiphany. It is nothing anywhere so soulful or enriching as that.

He is just up here to say goodbye. That's all there is on this rooftop for him tonight. It seems pretty empty and pointless after all this time, being as old and experienced as he is and yet being reduced to this, climbing all over creation like a kid on a playground, looking for something to amuse him and give him some sort of thrill, lift him up from all this discontent that wants to make him lay down with it and give up, and so he looks off at the city and the lights and the dark sky above for an answer, waiting for something to come. It may be a long time coming, he thinks. He turns to look back at the new store again, to make some sort of effort to determine his place within it, and his foot slips on a tiny sheen of loose pebble on the roof surface and a gust of west wind hits him in the face and moves him ever so slightly. He loses his balance—maybe he's a little off-kilter after all, he thinks, maybe he's more ripped than he previously believed—and when he reaches for the railing it is not where he thinks it is and he takes hold of the night air instead and knows how he is no bird with feathers and the sky is never going to hold him steady up here.

God, he thinks as he goes over the side.

He falls.

He thinks about dying all the way down, wondering how the world will possibly be able to exist without him in it. He imagines what it will be like in the morning, all the guys coming in to work, all the shoppers flocking through the doors to buy up what is left of the inventory. He thinks of the regular customers he has come to know through the years, how they will come in one last time to look around and say goodbye, how they will know as well as him that things will never be the same, how the new store will never treat them as good as the old store did, the new employees will never be as helpful and friendly as the old ones, it will all be different whichever way you slice it, and that's the way it is and there's not too much anybody can do about it. He thinks about how it is now and how it is going to be in the future all the way down, waiting and knowing in his mind how it will all go away for good when he hits the ground.

It is not the sharp impact he expects when the ground comes up to meet him, nor does all the light of the world go suddenly out as he enters into another realm. It is more like he hears a wave-like whoosh go up toward the region from where he has just entered, and his body actually sinks and ricochets like a red rubber ball, and in the midst of it he hears the song lyric say how he'll come bouncing back to you, whoever in the hell you is. In a moment he has stopped his vertical movement and feels himself settling into his environs, and he wonders if all the dead experience this feeling first and foremost, if this is their initial introduction to taking up residence on the other side.

After about a minute he starts to figure out that he may not be dead just yet, he may not be completely checked out and off for the hereafter after all. His nose detects the aroma of something distasteful, and against his cheek he can feel something oozing and sticky intertwining with his skin. When he wiggles his toes one after the other he can feel something mysterious attached to him and knows it is rubbing up against something hard through his shoes. He opens his eyes and makes out objects and colored shapes around him, moves his hand to touch them and feels something sharp prick his fingers. Glass, he thinks. Sour milk. He wipes his cheek and comes away with something akin to cottage cheese. Darkness is around him, but when he looks up he sees the sky, a star here, the quarter moon there. He reaches into the darkness and feels metal and iron, and all at once he knows where he is.

He is not in hell, he is not in heaven. He has fallen into a pretty damn full dumpster.

He is fairly well disgusted at what he's smelling and what's been smeared into his body, so he forgets for a moment to thank God for not being dead and gone and instead says words of praise and thankfulness like Shit and Goddamn and Christ, then gathers himself some with a better late than never sigh of relief at not truly being obliterated and history before deciding it would be a good idea to try and get out of this current domain he's suddenly become a part of.

The problem is when he starts to move his right arm pain shoots through him like lightning and hot smoke, and then he finds he can't bend it or straighten it out and he knows it is broken. He tries to turn over on his side and it's the hardest thing he's ever done outside of surviving his sad foolish marriage and the divorce that followed it, and so he has to inch himself around to where he can use his left arm for leverage and pull himself up sideways that way. Somehow via a miracle from God he manages to take hold of the dumpster's top (thank Jesus it is open) and hoist himself to his feet to where his head sticks out and he can see the back dock even through the darkness and see his car parked about ten yards away and see out toward the back lot where the south corner of the store ends. If he can make it there he can get to the door, use his key to go inside and call for help. He can call Miller. He can call an ambulance.

This is if he can get out of this damn dumpster. He's been pretty trashy in his life, he'll admit it, but he doesn't see why he has to be relegated to taking up permanent quarters in here with all the other refuse. Good god, he thinks, what a fucking mess. This is no damn way to end the year. He's got to get out of here somehow. He gets to work digging out with the one good arm he's got left.

SATURDAY, DECEMBER 31

On this last day of the year and the last time he will ever punch a time clock at the soon to be extinct Overton's Market, Phillip finds himself tapping his finger on the knees of his jeans as he rides along in John's truck on the way in for this final day of work. The sound of Steely Dan emanating from the dashboard seeps into his head like a salve he's needed to alleviate some unknown irritant for a while, and it is good to have a feeling of happiness and a willingness to get to work before actually arriving. Every facet of life truly is a state of mind, he thinks. Once you lift yourself up and take a look around at what's getting you down you generally get better. You somehow talk yourself off the ledge.

The first thing this morning he'd looked at Janet and told her he was ready to go home and he'd like to wake up very soon in the new year in his own bed. For the first time in a while, it seemed he'd uttered the right words to her, because all at once he could sense they weren't at war with each other anymore. It was like she'd decided he had chosen her and family life over his old friends and the life he'd once led.

He wasn't so sure exactly if that was totally it, but he knew he'd made some sort of decision. He knew he'd turned a corner somehow.

"You're never going to guess what I did last night," John says.

"Let me make a crazy stab. You got drunk and fell down the stairs?" "No, that's close to an every night thing. This was something really off the beaten path."

John takes a swallow of coffee from his travel cup and looks over and makes a lunatic face. "I got a wild hair and went by Carol's house."

"And you're out of the hospital already? That bulletproof vest of yours must really be high quality."

"We actually went out and ate pizza. She drank wine and I drained a few beers and we both had a good time. It was like we were on a date. We were almost acting as if we liked each other."

"Well, god, we can't have that."

"I'm really considering moving back, Phillip."

"That's the second time I've heard you say that. Heck, I always thought you liked it up there in the Far Country. I thought you were getting rich and didn't want to change anything."

"I work fifty hours a week, buddy, sometimes more. Once I get off there's nothing to do but come home. I'm always too tired to go anywhere—as if there's anywhere to go anyway. A few more years of it and I'll be nothing but an old man. I'm telling you, Phillip, a guy's life has got to be worth something when it's all said and done, or nothing he's done or any amount of money he brings in ever adds up to anything much. And I'm getting sick and tired of knocking myself out for a sum total of nothing."

Phillip is unused to having a philosophical conversation like this with John. It has been a long time since one has occurred between the two of them, maybe since high school or late nights at college in their dorm room—it's hard to pin it down—but it's been a while, more than a week for sure. He is surprised at what John has said, amazed, almost, at the fact that one of his friends has gazed upon the life parade going by and decided to do something about it other than standing like a cigar store Indian and watching it pass. It is like he and John have been traveling different avenues for a time but now seem to be pulling into a new town together at the same time. It is a nice feeling of understanding and kinship, an unexpected moment shared, something he'd decided a few ages ago would never happen again.

"That sounds good, buddy," he says. "Do you think you and Carol are going to get back together?"

"I don't know," John says. "It's possible. I'm not going to tell you yea or nay. I guess it all depends on whether she's completely lost her mind these days or not."

***

This last day of the year in Abington. Morning of northwest wind and the worst of winter on the way. David thinking how if he lived in the north he would be accustomed to all this frigidity and not be so damn cold, riding down Ballard Street gripping frosty handlebars, fingers numb even with gloves on. Couldn't find a stocking hat this morning and so he is hatless, what hair he has blowing in the breeze. Could stop and buy one but most places not open yet. And if he was a Yankee he wouldn't know what a season was, would just be cold constantly and angry about it all the time and not even know it, not even know he was mad, he would just be pissed off naturally that way without thinking about it.

It has been a while since David has been on a bicycle—maybe it was all the way back when he delivered papers in the summer to earn money to go to school, to buy a car—but it is all coming back to him now after some practice, after riding in the lot and pedaling back to his apartment through the traffic lights and four way stops. He'd had to carry the bike up the stairs at the apartment because he didn't have a chain and a lock to keep it outside and knew someone would steal it, it would be gone in the morning, and so he'd lugged it up the stairs and inside the door and set it in the floor in front of the television and the stereo, even washed off the seat with some dish soap and wiped off dust and remnants of cobwebs from sitting in John's garage so many years. The more he looked at it and put his hands on it the more he liked it. He decided he would gather some money up and pay John for it, and then it would be his. He was already not missing the Caravan. He was not missing Abington Home and Hardware either.

The thing he likes the best, after he begins to get used to the wind and the cold and doesn't have to think about it anymore, is this freedom type of feeling he has in his head that tells him he doesn't have to stop at red lights or obey signs or anything the normal people of Abington stuck inside their automobiles have to do. He can keep going and pass them silently with just the whir of his wheels making their slight hissing sigh as he goes by. He wonders if it's against the law not to have a helmet and if the police are going to pull him over if they see him, but in his mind he sees how he is empowered now to cut through a yard or go between cars and disappear down an alley and be so swift and elusive no one would ever be able to catch him. They would have to give up and watch him pedal away because he is so nimble and fast.

All this goes through his brain and he is grinning like a lopsided idiot when he gets to the store and sees Miller unlocking the door and knows he is right on time. He rides through the electric door and makes a circle on the front end like he is Roy Rogers on Trigger, and then pedals down the dairy aisle to park his bike in the backroom.

It is my bike, he thinks. I am going to pay John for it and devote some time to learning how to be happy.

***

Miller thinks one of these days he might just change his mind, sometime after he's found some balm with an abundance of drink and pot and some time away from all that is this final day so much, but he has his doubts. It might become something of a temptation in the near future to reveal how he has spent so many early mornings over the years at Overton's in the company of Bill the Friendly Grocery Ghost, sensing his presence, capitulating to his otherworldly designs, being the victim of pranks and signs and messages from the Great Beyond, or wherever it is Bill likes to call his home base these days. He might just let everyone know how these hauntings or visitations or contacts, or whatever it is the ghost hunters call them, are things he is going to miss as much as anything about the old store. He will probably want to pose the question to all those who might possibly understand, to ask them where they think old Bill might go now that the store he loved so much will be finally taken from him and reduced to rubble. Will he turn angry? Will he curse the new store? Take up residence somewhere inside the shiny appurtenances and make every day and venture the Overton family takes from here on out unlucky? Cause the place to suffer doom and fail?

Miller is right there with Bill. He is angry too. Foul deeds and desecration is what this all amounts to, he thinks, and I don't know if Bill or I can be persuaded to let these people get away with it. A few other things too on the agenda, he might add, like this old store closing is the only thing there is to worry about right now.

The phone call had come a little before midnight. It wasn't like he had been sound asleep or anything like that, but it also wasn't like he was expecting to have to get up and go down to the store and take Sammy to the emergency room. It's not that he's a bad friend or anything, and he's sorry Sammy has fallen and broken his arm and banged himself up, but, then, he wasn't the one who told the damn fool to climb up on the roof and risk his neck to begin with. He's glad Sammy didn't break his frigging neck, for sure, glad he didn't kill himself doing such a dumbass thing, but he also wouldn't mind kicking his best friend's ass right now, if it wasn't for the fact that Sammy has already had his ass kicked pretty good by the fall and the dumpster and the whole damn night in general.

So, no sleep much last night. Fine. Lack of sleep is something he's learned how to deal with over the years, all those times of working until eleven or twelve and being back in before the chickens. He does it better than anyone. But today he's had his sights on for a long time now, and today he wanted everything to be special. He wanted to be able to fully concentrate on this end of times thing. He didn't need a bunch of silly-ass distractions popping up around him clouding his sight, because god knows there are always plenty of shit missiles flying around his head anyway, so he doesn't need stuff like Sammy taking a tumble or Laurel calling him on the phone to discuss the possibilities of potential parenthood and banging on his door in the middle of the night. On all this he has to agree with old Will Shakespeare—none of this sort of crap happens along as a single spy; the whole lot seems to come along in great battalions, one after another and sometimes at the same time with guns a-blazing.

He unlocks the doors and flips the power switch at the top. Up the walk comes John and Phillip carrying take-out cups of coffee from McDonald's. David precedes them inside, pedaling his bike through the In door like he's getting in shape for an upcoming race. Sammy is sitting in the front office with his arm in a cast, bandages and bruises on his head and neck like he's the Frankenstein monster escaped from the ruins of some castle who has stopped here to smoke and drink wine and watch the day's festivities, beginning right now. Customers coming through the door and grabbing carts, pushing down the aisles, scooping up anything in sight. Here we go, Miller thinks. Everybody jump in a check lane, all help on the front, this is just like old times.

One-armed Sammy tries to come down and help bag, but he can't get the bags open with just his left hand and so has to lean on the check stands and talk to the long-time customers coming through. Miller and Phillip grab their old faithful lanes and start checking with the two borrowed cashiers, four lanes open with one to spare if it really gets bad, run these folks through, get them out before they have time to congest. Keep them moving and don't worry about stuff like accuracy or if everything in the basket gets scanned or not. Just get it into bags and out the door. Thanks for your business down through the years. No need to come back. Nothing for you to buy here anymore. Hope you got it while you could. Because if you don't see it now you never will. And it sure as hell ain't going to be here tomorrow.

Happy New Year.

All morning it is like there is snow in the forecast or an atomic bomb is on its way or there will never again be the opportunity to buy canned beans or frozen pizza or toilet tissue or any of the things that make life magical at half price ever again. When the lines start thinning, Miller notices they get shorter in the borrowed cashiers' lines but in he and Phillip's lines they keep coming, swarming, pressing forward, making sure, Miller thinks, that when they leave this place they are taken notice of and thanked and get to exchange their mode of currency with a familiar face, and so they choose Miller and Phillip to check them out and Sammy and John and David to bag their groceries, certain they are a part of history when they do this, that they will not be forgotten somehow when the bulldozers come and wipe away the history of this plot of earth where once they shopped, where once they walked and talked, year after year until today when suddenly it all comes to an end.

***

By noon the surge of early customers has passed. The aisles are empty of people and the shelves are sparse and barren in spots. Miller and Sammy walk the aisles, looking at areas where some exhausted soul could crawl into the empty space and sleep comfortably, and they can both tell that it won't take long for the moving and salvage crews to come in and load up what's left and strip the place of anything that can be used later or sold at auction or for scrap. Maybe it might take a day, perhaps longer; three days max would be a good bet.

"This is depressing," Sammy finally denotes.

"No shit," says Miller. "It's going to be hard to be around for everything that's fixing to happen."

"I guess God did me a favor having me take a dive off the roof. At least this way I'm not going to have to be here in the middle of everything helping out. I guess I'll just stand around with my cast and watch. I don't look forward to that shit either. Crap, Miller, I'd just as soon have died from the fall than have to be around here looking at all this shit going down."

"Some people are just too damn crazy to kill," Miller says. "You happen to be one of them."

While they're standing observing the desolation, Miller hears his name called on the intercom, so he heads back to the front prepared to deal with some customer wanting what is already reduced to the bone to be reduced even more, who won't truly be happy until whatever it is they want is given to them free, but when he turns the corner to where the check lanes are he sees Laurel standing by the first register talking to Phillip and John. David is sitting on the last lane eating a candy bar, grinning at Miller as he walks up, wearing this smile that says I know what you did, we all know what you've been doing, and we've all known everything about it since it first began.

Miller, being in love as he keeps telling himself he is somehow required to be in this situation, is still not too happy about seeing the supposed object of his affections and passions standing here in his territory when she really ought to be over at the new store with the man she said I Do to, doing some form of fastidious labor (maybe, he thinks, he should use a different term, forget that labor business) to insure the new Overton's has a smooth and successful opening next week. Miller has already had one long telephone conversation with Laurel last night, and that ought to be enough. When he left to collect Sammy from near-death and take him to the emergency room, Laurel had been by and visited his house, left a note, and then kept calling afterward. When he returned, desperate for sleep, he heard his doorbell, heard the knocking, laid there in bed until it went away, thinking of Laurel outside his door, Sammy in the spare bedroom, both of them requiring something from him he was too empty to dole out. He can't keep the old store open for Sammy. He can't make Laurel not be perhaps expecting and married to Jim. He's tried to keep all these things from becoming realities in their own times and places, but he's failed. The store is closing today. Four more hours and it's done. Laurel married Jim eight years ago and now here comes a baby and maybe it's his and maybe it's not. At this point he's wondering if it makes a difference. Nothing is going to change from back in the past to today to the end of next week, the first week of a new year. It is a done deal in the spin of the planet, all of it, and that's it. He tried to tell her as much last night, talking himself blue in the face until the wee small hours of the morning, but she kept opening up new possibilities and vistas for the two of them, like all this new twist of plot concerning a baby is something that is going to be worked out over the phone and everybody's going to live happily ever after. Had it not been for Jim coming in at last from god knows where so far into the night they might still be talking, working out their sunny Cinemascope ending where Laurel gives up her comfortable monied life for love and everybody lives happily ever after. "I came by to see if you might want to go to lunch," she says. Laurel doesn't care if Phillip or John or David hears what she says. She knows this is no secret to any of them and hasn't been for a long time. She's past the point of being careful anymore.

"I can't right now," he tells her. "I've got too much to do. Running out of time to get things done, you know."

"Why don't you just let it go," she says. "There's nothing around here that's going to go anywhere. There aren't any customers and there aren't going to be any more either. It's New Year's Eve, Miller— everybody's shopping at real stores by this time, buying all their stuff for their parties. Nobody's going to come in this old place. Heck, there's nothing here left to buy. You could go ahead and lock the doors up right now and it wouldn't make the slightest bit of difference."

"It would to me. You know we can't leave early," he smiles. "After all, all us folks are paid by the hour over here, and poor folks like us can't afford to lose any time. We have to get our hours in. No hours, no pay, you know how it goes." He doesn't really want to be mean like this, but he goes ahead and says it anyway. "Maybe if good old Jim and your wealthy in-laws paid us a little more then it could be some of us worker bees might be able to take a little time off and enjoy ourselves every blue moon or so."

"I didn't know you were at the poverty level, Miller. You should have spoken up."

"I don't like to dwell on my low position in society too much, Laurel. The rich get rich and the poor try to get time and a half--that's just the way it goes, you know, first your money, then your clothes." He takes a stray bascart and rolls it with a flick of his wrists toward a line of carts stacked up by the front window. This is one of his tricks he's learned to do through years of practice. At the last minute the bascart curves with backspin and nestles into the row of parked carts like magic. There's nothing in this store he can't do, but it doesn't matter now, he can see that. "Besides," he says, "this is the last day for this place, and there are a few of us around here this old store actually means something to, who want to be around to send the old girl out in style. Lunch," he tells her, "is one of those things I can do anytime, Laurel. Lunch can wait." Lunch and everything else, he thinks. Lunch and all the fixings can maybe wait forever and it still might never be time for it even then. He can see this notion of being secondary registering with Laurel by the way her eyes look at him and then slowly blink in some sort of comprehension. She studies him like the possibility exists that they have never in this lifetime met before.

***

At three o'clock it looks like all the business is truly gone for good, so Miller sends his two borrowed checkers home early so they can get a good head start on their own New Year's Eve revels, gets rid of them primarily so he can be surrounded during these final two hours by his four comrades in crime, who grew up here and have some sort of appreciation for what is happening at the moment and it won't have to be explained to them in detail about how this moment in the time they're in actually means something in the grand scope of things. At the risk of getting too sentimental but at the same time not wanting to leave anything unsaid, he brings out a cardboard box from the office he's been saving for this moment, folding back the top flap to reveal bottles of wine and champagne and a community-sized bottle of Irish Whiskey, the contents a collection he's splurged on at the liquor store a few weeks back, knowing this day was coming and making damn certain he wouldn't have to go through it unarmed and in his right mind.

God forbid.

David, as his new personality deems, is the first to help himself to a heaping glass of Chablis in a red disposable plastic cup. He fills it to the brim as if it is some drink from an elementary school carnival, takes a healthy sip and swallows it like a parched canine just back inside the house from a long romp. Sammy watches him gulp his helping down the hatch and thinks how, if his damn right arm wasn't in a cast right now, he would get a sharpie and go draw a smiling Kool-Aid face on David's cup, just because David is acting like such a kid with his new taste for wine. Sammy knows it won't take that long for old Davey Boy to be knocked back on his ass—closing time, tops—but hell's bells, the guy's been a frigging tee-totaler for all the good years of his life, so he's got a lot of catching up to do. Besides, with two busted marriages and a wrecked car and starting the new year off unemployed, David probably needs to be out of his gourd for a little while just to keep from getting depressed and taking a leap off a roof somewhere. But I did that, Sammy thinks. On purpose or accidental, it doesn't matter much. It happened, so who am I to pass judgment?

"Here's to this old store," says David. He raises his cup up toward the ceiling and the fluorescent lights, like maybe Zeus is up there somewhere watching over this mythical place from the clouds. "I'm damn glad to be here today. The dumbest thing I ever did was quit working here in the first place."

"You've done some pretty dumb shit, David," Miller tells him. "You may need to re-think that for a minute and make sure you're not forgetting something."

"We could probably come up with a pretty extensive list," Phillip says.

"I'm not going to argue with you," David smiles. "You're probably right." He pours himself another Goliath serving. "I'm going to agree with you on everything right now, Miller, old buddy, old pal, because I don't want you or your one-armed buddy over there to get mad at me. Cause I need a favor. I need a job, fellows. I need you gents to get me on at the new store. I don't care what I do, just don't make me go back to the mean ol' AHH no more."

"I'm pretty sure you don't have to worry about AHH calling you in for an interview or taking you back on their own," Sammy says. "Their re-hire policy probably isn't spacious enough to have a clause in it for your return."

"I really hate that for me," says David.

Phillip and John stick their heads out the door for a temperature check, but the wind is blowing and it's too cold to stand outside and see what's happening in the world of Abington, so they duck back in and look out the glass at the empty lot.

"Remember how we used to sit in lawn chairs out back by the dock on summer nights drinking beer until the cows came home?" Phillip strains his eyes looking down the walk, like he might spot the youthful apparitions of the lot of them out there in their joint glory, holding their cans of Schlitz and Blatz and Pabst Blue Ribbon. He doesn't see anyone, but he knows phantoms are back there somewhere and will for certain appear at some point soon. This is, after all, the afternoon of Store Ghosts Past, so nothing is off the table. "We'd load our trunks down with coolers full of ice and beer, sit out there singing and laughing listening to the radio and getting good and drunk. How we avoided getting arrested I'll never know."

"We had a system," John says, "our early warning plan. We'd sit back there around the second corner of the building where we could see headlights flashing off the wall if a car was coming, and the wall hemmed the sound in to where we could hear them coming too. Everybody sat close to the dumpster so you could throw your beer can away if a car actually did come. We'd shut the car trunks too, so if it was the cops they wouldn't be able to see what we had. It worked like a charm every time."

"Happened a few times," Miller laughs. "The cops would pull up and we'd be sitting there in our chairs chatting with halos over our heads like perfect angels. Just got off work, we'd tell them, and shooting the bull before we go home. I don't think they ever believed us but they couldn't catch us in the act of doing anything illegal. I think after a while they got tired of trying. I guess there was more important shit for them to worry about."

A long brown Buick pulls up in the lot and parks. Nobody gets out for a minute, and everyone sits with their beverages and wonders if this is an actual customer or if this old gas-guzzling turdy-looking Buick Wildcat is out of fuel and just needs a place to repose for the night.

An old guy in an ancient topcoat walks up to the glass and peers inside. The wind lifts what sparse gray hair he still has on his head up and down, and he cups his hands around his temples to see if he can spot any activity going on inside.

"Will you look at this shit?" says Sammy. "It's Jack."

"Goddamn Jack," says Miller. "I thought this son of a bitch was dead by now."

They all know Jack Lawson, since Jack is the one who first hired them on as a group so many moons back. The store had gone through a new remodel then, and they'd all gone in and applied the week after school started their sophomore years, two weeks before the doors got opened with a councilman cutting a ribbon, and Jack, who was the head clerk and a good friend of old Mr. Overton, took a look at the five of them and hired them all right there on the spot, asking them only one question, do you boys want to make some money, and they'd said yes. Be here at three tomorrow, he'd told them. Don't be late or I'll look you up and kick your skinny asses.

Jack still has a limp when he walks. That's from somebody—it wasn't one of them—who accidentally slammed into his ankle with a motorized power jack. Knocked the hell out of old Jack, they remembered. His ankle was probably broken and his foot turned a strange shade of blue (*he used to take his shoe and sock off and show it to us, rub it with his fingers for a minute, then it was back on with the sock and shoe and back to work*) and he never went to the doctor for it. Never missed a goddamned day. They were sixteen, seventeen then, and none of them liked adults much. Thought they were most of the time absolutely full of shit, always trying to tell them how to do something, tell them how they were always dead wrong, but Jack wasn't that way. Jack just said, come on, let's do it, let's get this sucker done. They counted themselves lucky when they got scheduled to help Jack on a work day. They would have almost worked for free those days. They all liked Jack.

Jack walks in the door and looks at the five of them sitting on the check lanes and standing around by the windows.

"Don't look like too much has changed around this goddamned place," he says. "You guys don't look like altogether worthless sissies anymore, but you seem to still be pretty good at hanging around getting not a goddamn thing done when there's probably a hundred things that needed doing an hour ago."

"We've been waiting for you to show up and tell us where to start," says Miller.

"The way this damn place looks I should have come in a couple of years ago."

Everybody's up to shake Jack's hand, pat him on the back and stand grinning at each other. This is the way this store ought to be, they think; if it was this way all the time there'd be no reason for it to close, because it couldn't get any better. There'd be no room for improvement.

"I saw that goddamn poor excuse for a building they've put up across the way," Jack says. "Old man Overton would shit in his grave if he was to get a look at that place. It looks to me like if a big goddamned wind comes along it will blow the whole thing down." He looks around the store, up at the ceiling and down the aisles. "This place here they'll have to bring in the Enola Gay and drop a bomb on to bring it down completely. This is one tough old piece of construction. I hate to see it get torn down."

"We ain't decided if we're going to let it happen yet," Sammy says. "We may form a human chain and not let the bulldozers come in."

"What did you do to your arm?" Jack looks at Sammy's cast. "Did you lose at arm wrestling or something?"

"I fell off the roof," Sammy grins.

"Like I say, looks like not much has changed around here. Once a dumbass, always a dumbass." He sees the bottles lined up on the check stands and everybody with cups in their hands. Jack has always liked to drink. His eyes light up.

"My doctor will probably kick my ass for this, but give me some of whatever it is you kids are drinking."

Jack holds out a cup while David sloshes red wine into it, filling it up to the brim like it is bug juice and they are all at summer camp. Jack sniffs at it and scrunches up his nose like he's had better, but takes a big drink anyway.

"It's been fifteen years since I've been inside this place," he says, looking around at the walls and the front display bunkers sitting empty in front of him. "It's funny how it looks exactly the same. I can't tell if it's even been painted again or not."

"Probably hasn't been," Miller says. "If it has, I had nothing to do with it, and I sure don't remember anybody else taking on the job."

"I probably spot-mopped the front end once or twice," John says. "That's about as much as I could do. I've been under a lot of stress for a long time now."

Sammy laughs at something dancing around in his head.

"Jack, do you remember those times when we'd lock up early and strip the floors? You were in charge of running the buffer and the rest of us were moving displays and swinging mops and laying down stripper and hot water and wax as fast as we could. Everybody kept slipping and falling and busting their asses all night long."

"We raided the cooler and polished off about a case of beer every time," Phillip laughs.

"Two cases," Jack says. "That's why everybody was always falling down. It wasn't from the slippery shit on the floor."

They talk about ancient store history for a while, drinking wine and beer and passing around a big bottle of Bushmill's. When it gets later in the afternoon Jack says he needs to go, his wife will be looking for him, he doesn't like to drive when it gets to be twilight because he just doesn't see like he used to, and he's shaking hands with all his old boys when Miller remembers how Jack always used to sing when he worked.

"Jack, do you still sing that song 'Goodnight, Irene' like you used to?"

"I belt it out it in the shower every goddamn morning. Always been my favorite."

They all start singing. It's been water under the bridge and miles down the road and everybody's looped, but they remember the all the words with no problem.

Goodnight, Irene, Goodnight, Irene…

Jack drives away in his Buick and they stand on the sidewalk with their arms locked still singing their asses off looking up at the rising moon. It's coming up on five o'clock and the sun's already down like it's the middle of the night and it's time to lock the door. This is it for the old girl.

"At the risk of getting hokey and sentimental," Miller announces, "I'm claiming the right to be the last customer this store ever has. Therefore, I'm buying this Mars Bar here. Who wants to be the last official checker?"

"I do," says Phillip. He jumps behind his register in Lane Five.

"I'll be the last official bagger," says David. "You guys come through for me and I can also be the first official bagger at the new store."

"What a fucking honor that will be," Sammy says. Phillip punches in the price of the candy bar and Miller hands him a dollar bill. 1-0-0, cash tendered, and the drawer opens. Phillip hands Miller his change, and Miller takes the receipt and puts it in his billfold. Something to look at later on down the line.

The door is locked and the sign gets turned off above the door. All that's left to do now is take the money from the tills and what's left in the safe and drop everything into a big bank bag, one with a lock, then carry it over to the new store. No need for any accounting or sorting change and bills or bundling checks and food stamps. That's all over now. Just put it in the bag and be done with it. No need for it to be here anymore. The last thing is for everyone to head to the clock in the back and punch out, bring their timecards to the front and hand them to Miller, so he can put them in the money bag and take them over to the new store too, because their cards don't have any place here either. Nothing here to do anymore for anybody to have to clock in for. Nobody is in a hurry to go to the back. Nobody's busting their ass to get out the door and start celebrating New Year's Eve.

"I guess we could do a few verses of 'Kumbaya,'" Sammy offers.

"I've sang enough for now," says David. "A little bit more and I'll have to barf again. I'm not used to this alcoholic life yet."

"Keep practicing," John says. "You'll be all right."

It's about an hour more before anyone leaves. Phillip starts the process by saying he's got to get back to his in-laws' house for dinner, and John, perhaps the straightest of the quintet, says he's got to go too. He has plans. Just a date, he says, nobody needs to get too excited and start reading anything into it.

They read into it anyway. They know John too well, know something strange and out of the norm is going on with him somehow. They don't worry about it too much; it's one of those things that will reveal itself to them later, just like everything else among them has always stood up and taken a bow since the beginning of time as they know it. None of them has ever been much good at keeping secrets from each other.

"I've never pedaled a bike home on New Year's Eve and been blind-running at the same time," says David. "Life's like a new adventure all the time now."

"Think of all you've been missing all these years," says Sammy. "Repeat after me, alcohol is my friend."

Miller has to take the money bag to the new store. Sammy rides over in the Sun Bug with him so no bandits can waylay him and make off with the last of the old store's profits. He doesn't go so far as to go up with Miller to the door and keep him safe that far, but just sits in the Sun Bug and waits for him to come back. Sammy has seen enough of the new store already and doesn't need to refresh his memory of it just yet.

He fiddles with the radio while he waits, hears the Pointer Sisters sing 'Jump'.

Miller doesn't stay long. Jim is the only one up in the office, so Miller hands the bag to him and gives him a quick salute, like he's in the Luftwaffe or something, and then turns and takes off out the door before any conversation about how the last day went can get started. He knows this is not the correct thing to do right this moment, this rejection of protocol and good will and team harmony with measured silence, but he doesn't care. He doesn't want to talk about the last day of the old store or anything else. There will be plenty of time to talk later. Besides, he's seen Laurel's car parked outside, so he knows she's still around somewhere. He can talk to her later too, but not tonight.

Maybe next year he can begin some of these conversations, he thinks, if he can only clear his docket. Maybe it can be his New Year's resolution to chat a little with the two Overtons at some point before this time next year. Then again, maybe a year might be a bit too soon, pushing things a little.

"I hate to be a party-pooper on New Year's Eve, but I think I'm going to sack out for a while." Sammy looks out the windshield at the town going by, folks in cars heading to parties or to clubs or countdown gatherings, the year passing in one direction while he and Miller go in another. "Whatever this painkiller crap is that they gave me, I'm pretty sure you're not supposed to mix it with alcohol." He looks over at Miller and grins. "Whoops," he says. "Fucked up again."

Miller watches Sammy make his way to his Vette, feeling almost like maybe he ought to follow Sammy home to make sure the guy can open his apartment door with one hand while he's pretty much out of his mind, but then he drives away, leaving Sammy to make it as best he can while he and his Sun Bug head out for who knows where. The fact that it is New Year's Eve runs through his mind for about the trillionth time, and he wonders if there is going to be any peace he can find anywhere the rest of the night to circumvent this newest unwanted obsession. The idea of going home doesn't seem so sweet to him, and the vision in his mind's eye of sitting in some bar or tavern listening to music and drinking by himself—which is generally the select company he most desires lately— doesn't appeal to any part of him whatsoever. He hears the click of the Sun Bug's tiny engine coursing through the back seat, hears the whir of the tires, and thinks how he could just head for the highway and motor off somewhere, take some kind of unscheduled road trip in his little yellow Nazi car, but then he thinks how he would be caught in the middle that way, how it would be New Year's Eve and he would be out on the road ticking the miles and the minutes to midnight away, and if he drank to get a good happy buzz he might get pulled over, and if he didn't he might run into someone who was both drinking and driving and not doing a very good job of it. It is Amateur Night, he decides, and because of it wherever he travels during this night's twists and turns he is going to be taking a chance either way.

He thinks of the unfinished bottle of Bushmills still sitting on the first check stand back at the store, the bottles of varying levels of wine surrounding it, the leftover beer in the cooler that hasn't sold. He thinks of the compactly-rolled joint in the inside pocket of his jacket, how there was a part of him this morning that already knew this night was going to come to this and told him to go ahead and load himself for bear. He thinks of the old store standing on its last night, alone, unattended, cast off from the lessons it had taught its denizens through the years, the glory it had known. Soon it would not be standing. Soon it would be gone.

He knows where he needs to be

The lights are turned off, but he doesn't need them. He could find his way around inside this building blindfolded, even if he and John Milton were twins. He hadn't set the alarm when he'd left, since there was nothing inside really left to steal, so he doesn't have to punch in the entry code. Remember it forever, he thinks, like my first phone number. Never go away. 1-9-6-6. Year I started working here. Set the number in myself when it got installed those years ago, looking at the manual. Somehow me doing it meant the place was mine.

There's no music playing over the P.A., and that's good. When it's quiet like this he can hear the central heat ticking, the coolers clicking off and on by thermostat, even the traffic from Clement Avenue seventy-five yards away going north and south, all the cars and drivers and passengers on their way to some form of festivity. Walking down the produce aisle he hears tapping and knocking coming from the front door up by the office and the checkout lanes. He stops and swallows a mouthful of whiskey but does not turn to go and answer the summons. He wonders if it is Laurel, off from work at the new store, seeing his car here and wanting to talk and get this thing that is between them straight before the calendar year gets flipped. He hopes it is her out there knocking, but he does not want to go and see for himself. If he goes and it is not her he will be disappointed. If he goes and it is actually her standing there he will be trapped into some sort of moment of truth. For now, he would rather have his imagination rule the night. He is happy to avoid any sign of real life going on outside these walls for a while longer.

The tapping stops and he is cloaked in delicious silence again. He leans against what once was a weigh station for bulk produce and studies the empty shelves around him, the Pepsi machine in the corner with the lights blinking on all the selections denoting there is no can of any flavor available. Beside it is the decrepit water fountain, old as the store itself, so old and frequented that no amount of scrubbing or scouring could ever make it shine or appear clean. But it always worked, he thinks. The water stream shoots so high you don't have to bend over to get a drink, and the water is cold like it just came down from the mountains and makes your eyes water it tastes so good.

He walks over and takes a drink, washes the whiskey and wine and beer from this afternoon and tonight down.

(Fill my mouth and hold it there. If I swallow it down it's gone for good. Have to find some other place where I can get a drink like this.)

He hears the cooler door close back inside the swinging doors of the produce prep room, the whoosh of the rubber insulation meeting the jamb and the jangle of the iron handle clanking with the impact. He half expects the swinging doors to crash open and a cart laden with stock to come rolling out, boxes of lettuce, wrapped yellow squash in trays, bags of Cole slaw and salad mix, but nothing appears, and he knows what it is. It's Bill, that's all. Nothing to worry about. Bill has a few more things to get done around here

Miller is more than glad to know that on this last dark night he is not alone in here.

***

After John lets him out and drives off, Phillip stands in the front yard a moment before going in. What constitutes his family is inside this door and he needs just a moment to think and take a breath before entering into the vista of real life once again. As he sees John's taillights grow smaller and disappear around the corner he turns and looks at the house and thinks about how there once was a time about a thousand years ago when he would climb these same steps before him and ring the doorbell. In five seconds—almost instantly, like the automatic doors at the store—the front door would open and there would be Mrs. Adams standing there, some form of smile on her face, the kind of smile he has yet to figure out what it meant even to this night. He can walk up and open this door and see it again right now, and he is always going to have the same small question in the back of his mind when he focuses upon it.

Does she like me? Does she think her daughter made a good choice? Is she waiting for me to fuck everything up, so she and Mr. Adams can say to their daughter, we were afraid this was going to happen, sweetheart. We could see it coming right from the start.

It is not really like that and he knows it. This sort of reasoning, like since the first time he took a step, is what has been first and foremost in his head constantly, for as long as he can remember, warning him, telling him to be careful, to back off, to not jump into a current so strong he can't make it back to shore. Don't fall in love too deeply. Don't try too hard to be a good father. Never let your guard down. Whatever you do, it's a good chance you're going to fail. Don't let that ever escape your mind. The only ones to trust are your friends. They won't let you down. They will not abandon you.

But what it is, he thinks, looking up at the coal-black winter sky, is I have removed myself from all scenes, inch by inch, year by year, a digression imperceptible to anyone but myself. I am married, I have a daughter, I teach at a place I like. Everything is, as they say, hunky dorey, cool, about as good as it can be, but I am not truly there at all. I am not really a part of it. I am somewhere else.

I've come home for a week, circulated in my old town, worked my old job, been around the old friends I always knew were theoretically there for me, supposedly had my back, like folks tend to say these days. But it's a strange world here now, a familiar location filled with people I used to know, close strangers I know and don't know at the same time.

It is no one's fault, he thinks, this thin, imitation life he has forged. He is going to have to learn some way to live it without taking more backward steps, because if he doesn't watch it, then conversations and moments like he's having now out here alone on this winter night are going to become a regular routine. He doesn't want to be like this. He wonders what it was that steered him this way. Maybe he has spent too much time in some sort of regret for having to leave the past, for having a present that maybe wasn't quite what he'd wanted it to be, for seeing how the future was right there in front of him and from the sowing he had done up to then there wasn't too much of anything in the fields to be reaped.

He is going to have to do something different. It is time for a change. The old year is passing. The New Year is coming. He can almost hear its footsteps, coming up on him fast. It is time to get started, time to get it on the road.

He climbs the old familiar steps

Everyone is sitting in the living room when he walks in, Mr. and Mrs. Adams, Janet, his daughter, like they've been waiting for him to come home.

"Hi," he says. "Happy New Year."

***

John is wondering if maybe he's entered into his second childhood or something, if perhaps his testosterone levels have found new life and are bubbling up to the surface out of control. He drives his truck recklessly along the streets, almost as if he has imbibed too much and is behind the wheel out of control, but he knows that is not the case. He has actually been a pretty good boy this afternoon at the store, what with all the alcohol and weed present and every bit of it there for the taking. He had been careful to have only a beer here, a plastic cup of wine there, no whiskey whatsoever, and only two random tokes on the plentiful numbers that were flying around the store like planes buzzing the Empire State Building with King Kong perched on top. There had been something in his mind even then, even right from the beginning of the day, telling him how he would be wise to pace himself this day, to not work himself too hard or throw his damn back out in service to Overton's Market, because this was all going to dust sooner or later anyway and it is getting damn nigh time that all the old faithful—he and Phillip and Sammy and David, and even Miller, who, if he was Captain Smith would be going down with the ship here at the end--be best prepared to adopt the philosophy of every man for himself, because this store stuff is over and they are going to be the ones left behind when it sinks.

So John had risen from his bed this morning looking for a lifeboat to float away on.

In the last hour before closing he'd gone to the back office and called Carol. She answered on the first ring, like she'd been sitting beside the phone waiting for it to ring, and she had not acted too surprised when she heard his voice. He thinks about it now and deduces she would probably have been surprised only if he hadn't called. And he is not surprised he's called her and is heading her way. All at once it is like she has not been seeing anyone else and the years that have passed by did not contain a divorce or a separation or his moving away to McGinnis to work and beginning a new life away from her. He drives along listening to the radio, and it is like none of this has ever really happened.

It also doesn't surprise him one tiny little damn bit when she opens the door and instead of the two of them getting ready to brave the New Year's Eve crowds and go out for dinner somewhere they instead fall upon and into each other like this dining out business can just take a number and take a seat and wait, because for now the two of them are hungry for something no restaurant in town has on their menu, and if they have to wait until next year to actually eat, well, that will be okay by them too, because for this moment in this old year all they want is what their fingers are touching, what their lips are tasting, what they have been hungering for all along and didn't really know about until now.

***

David is still not the best in the world at this bike-riding thing, because he almost busts his ass coming through the gates of the complex going full speed like he knows he probably shouldn't be doing. He hits a clump of withered wet leaves and the wheels go almost sideways on the pavement and it's a damn miracle of God he doesn't lose it right there and smash into the brick wall by the entrance or go flying off the seat and bouncing off somebody's car. Somehow none of this happens, and he is able to coast down the hill and dismount from his trusty new aluminum steed and haul it up the stairs with him. He shuts the door and parks the bike in his living room in front of the television and the stereo, staggers somewhat into the kitchen and picks out a Hungry Man fried chicken dinner for supper, and sits down while it heats at his kitchenette bar, scene of all his feasts and meditative sessions.

Last meeting of the year, he thinks.

He finds the silence relaxing and enjoyable right now, especially after all the conversation and hubbub at the store on this closing day. It is nice to sit and not have to endure anything from the outside world. He has been through a lot over the past few days, quitting his job, wrecking the Caravan, riding a bicycle around and getting high and tipsy with no sense of limitation, but he all at once realizes he's come to the end of the trek or whatever journey he's been embarking on and it is nice to stop now and catch his breath before a new race begins again, perhaps as early as tomorrow. No, he thinks, tomorrow is New Year's Day, a Sunday, a holiday, a day to nurse hangovers and make resolutions and watch bowl games. He resolves to sleep in, maybe not leave the apartment all day. It depends on what he has here to eat. He may have to get on his bike and go to a store or a restaurant. Must check the old food supply, he thinks.

Some early bird begins shooting off firecrackers outside, unable to wait four more hours to begin making noise, and David sits for a moment wondering if this is going to go on all the way up to midnight and beyond. While he is pondering such unpleasantness, he hears another sound outside his door, a rhythmic sort of whimpering mixing in between the blasts and the bangs. He walks to the door and peers out the hole, sees nothing but the railing on the porch, then opens the door thinking maybe he'll scream at whoever the mad bomber is down in the lot and tell him to cool it for a while. When he looks down a gray kitten looks back at him from where it has taken shelter by the steps. The kitten, figuring it truly has nothing to lose by taking a chance, walks toward David's foot and stops at the toe of his Adidas, sniffs it and paws it like maybe it's been put there to save it.

David regards the kitten a minute, then against his judgment reaches down and picks it up.

"Are you a boy or a girl?" he asks. He thinks about what a kitten might be hungry for, if it's going to shit all over his apartment, what it might tear up with its claws if he doesn't watch it like a hawk.

He could put this animal down now and shut the door, go back in and eat his nourishing TV dinner all by his lonesome, and to hell with all this kind-hearted shit that seems to be wanting to overtake him. It's been a long couple of days.

He carries the kitten inside and closes the door.

***

Sammy finds it funny how even when the rare occasion arises when he wants to do the right thing, the sensible and rational thing, there is always something going down one way or another that seems to keep it from happening.

Take tonight, for instance.

Here he is, full of varying portents of alcohol, toked out of his skull, his system full of prescription painkillers for this busted arm he's managed to acquire, trying to do everything with his left arm and making a damn mess out of it, and all he wants to do is swallow down some dry Cheerios and chew up a Baby Ruth for supper and then sleep it off for as long as it takes for him to feel human again, and what happens but the phone starts ringing. He lets the answering machine pick up the message, and it's a female voice asking if he's there, telling him to pick up on his end, and the machine turns off and then the phone starts ringing again.

This keeps going on while he lounges in bed. He thinks about getting up and going in and turning off the ringer just so he can get a little peace, but he's so stoned and drunk and the phone is so damn far away. He stays in bed thinking maybe he'll get lucky and this electronic assault will eventually end, that all he has to do is let it run its course, but when he thinks he's done just that and he's on the victory side and can close his eyes and drift away in peace the pounding starts in on his door and he knows it's not going to go away anytime soon, maybe not go away at all, until he hoists himself up from the mattress and goes and sees what the goddamned fire is.

He opens the door not really knowing or giving much a shit about who might be standing there beating on his door. It is Mary Lynn Baldwin (he thinks that's her last name) standing in the hallway smiling at him, looking like she's really accomplished something by getting him to acknowledge her presence. It is not so much that he is not surprised to see her standing here, for she has been in his apartment before, a number of times, and he could not really, if pressed, give a definitive number of the times he's screwed her brains out before she had to go home to her husband, who is some dumbass Sammy has never seen before, never met, but who has to be a complete loser to be married to this slut, and of course Sammy knows he too is a real dipshit and dumbass for continuing to do the dirty deed with this Mary Lynn he flirted with and picked up in Aisle Three of the store when she makes herself available to him, but that's not anything new in the way he seems to live these days, and he hasn't quite got around just yet to grieving over how irresponsible and absolutely crappy his actions are when it comes to porking other mens' wives and assorted women who shop in the store or drink at a bar or just wherever he happens to go and this sort of shit starts to happen. He needs to straighten his ass up and fly right, but he hasn't been able to get around to it just yet.

"It's New Year's Eve, Mary Lynn," he says. "What in the hell are you doing here?"

"I came to see you. I didn't have anything else to do."

"Don't you and your husband have some party or big social event to go to? Looks to me like you two ought to be out on the town or something."

"Dennis? That son of a bitch? I haven't heard anything from him since he left for his damn bowl game this morning."

"Where's his bowl game at?"

"I don't know. Florida. North Carolina. Who gives a shit?"

Before he can come up with some sort of an excuse and close the door in her face, Mary Lynn pushes past him and moves into the apartment.

"What did you do to your arm?" she asks.

"A boa constrictor wrapped around it at work. It was hiding under one of the bunkers."

"I didn't know if you'd be home tonight or not," she says. She moves toward him, trying her best to be sexy and seductive. Sammy doesn't think she's doing much of a job. "I was hoping you were."

She starts trying to wrap around him, like she's kin to that snake he just told her about.

"I don't want to ruin your New Year's, but I'm not feeling so hot right now."

"I'll make you feel better real fast."

Before he knows it she is all over him there in the alcove between the kitchen and the living room and the two bedrooms down the hall, and he is having a hard time, one-handed as he is, fending her off. He has never that he knows of tried evading a woman before and finds his footwork and defensive strategies pretty poor, lacking a good bit in effectiveness in avoiding this aggressive form of pursuit. In spite of his aches and pains and over-consumption of alcohol and drugs, he still finds himself halfway liking it—he is sick like that--even if the other portion of his brain not jaded and crazed by artificial stimulation tells him he needs to stop and grow up and quit acting like he's the poster boy for the perpetuation of the last days of the Roman

Empire. I mean, god, Sammy, when is this shit going to stop? When are you going to ever grow up?

Not tonight, it appears.

He, of course, goes through with the dastardly deed. It occurs to him in the midst of the heaving and breathing and teeth-gritting and oh-gods and such that one of these days or nights he might want to go about all this in a different manner. Maybe he ought to try finding someone he likes and work his way up to this kind of thing gradually, flowers and perfume and all that jazz. Maybe it would be different and better that way.

Well, he thinks, I did that once. I used to think like that, be that way. But it's been a while. It was a long time ago.

When it's over, he falls back on the bed and looks at the ceiling fan above him. He wonders what time it is, how long it will be until the New Year gets rung in, if Mary Lynn, snoring beside him, will haul her ass up and be gone before that happens. He notes how this is the last time he will go to bed with someone in 1988.

He starts thinking about how he's not getting any younger. It's not exactly an original thought.

***

About halfway through this final tour of the store, Miller walks back into what once was the meat department cutting room and pours his cup of whiskey down the sink. Some subliminal message—sent from on high, he supposes—has come to him during his solitary excursion down the aisles and told him this evening would be better spent and bear more of an understanding if viewed with a sober eye and a clear mind. In his middle age he has not been as receptive to taking suggestions from anything outside the scope of his own self too much, but somehow tonight, with the occasion of the store's closing and all the upheaval that entails, he finds himself open for outside advice.

The whiskey swirls around the stainless-steel sink once, then flows down the drain.

(Sammy and I used to sneak off the front and come back here at night to talk to Randy. Stand here behind the one-way glass watching people leaning over the meat case looking at packages of pork chops, ground beef, chuck roasts all wrapped up in trays with the price stuck on the label. Blood dripping from the packages sometimes. People wiping their fingers on the rail. Every now and then see somebody peel off a reduced label from an old package getting ready to go out of date and stick it on a newer one. Take it up front and sneak it through for savings. Trained all our checkers to never say a word about it. Just ring in the regular price and go on. Knew the sneaky-ass customer would never say anything. And sometimes Randy would say, watch that lady. She's freezer-bound. Find the package she'd picked up later stashed in with the frozen peas. Buried beneath popsicles. Randy always right. And one day Randy walked out the door and didn't come back. Fired for stealing, we heard. Taking meat out the back door.

And Bill not the only spirit in here tonight. Can hear distant voices speaking to each other, baggers and checkers getting called to the front, beep of scanned items, click of keys, squeaky wheels on four-wheelers and cash drawers opening and closing. Old Miss Nora, slow as hell on the register. Jack back by the truck rail slicing boxes open with his cutter. Jim Overton bagging on the front end—what was it, two weeks? —then there he was in a register, then two weeks after that up in the office standing around with his finger up his ass peering out over the glass like he was some kind of crown prince. Groomed and prepped to take over someday, and someday came soon. Off to college and came back a manager. Then Laurel happened along. And I knew that was trouble right from the start. Four years, though, before I touched her. And that was only after she touched me. When she came up against me that day. In the back room standing by the dairy cooler. Her face so close and I couldn't stop. Happened before I knew it. And years go by and I keep growing older and I'm fucking the boss's wife and calling it love trying to make myself feel better like I'm in the right about it. And now there may be a consequence for it all, some fee I have to pay for calling something love that really wasn't what it was, and the fact of it being I knew it all along every step of the way.)

Miller doesn't keep count of how many times he laps the store, how many lost faces and voices Bill points out to him, what lessons and memories he carries with him that he never knew were there before, how many more years and holidays it will take before it is enough. He looks at the store before him, around him, the ceiling above his head, the world outside. This store is him. It has been him for a long time. Soon it will be gone.

He waits until it is officially midnight, then locks the doors and drives home. The Sun Bug's top is down and it's freezing cold like it ought to be on the first of January, but there's a part of him that hardly feels a thing.

NEW YEAR

No appearance by the sun yet. It was just the kind of gray, cloudy, dismal sort of morning that if you don't really have to be anywhere it doesn't seem to matter much at all if you pull the covers back over your worn-out, hungover head and sleep away as many hours as you can of it.

But by eleven Sammy is on the phone, calling everybody and saying, come on, I'm hungry, let's eat. Let's go to Dino's. Greasy food cures whatever it is that ails you.

By two-thirty there is perfect attendance. Sammy and Miller ride in together, David has managed to tear himself away from his new kitten and wobble over on his bicycle after going to an ATM to get twenty dollars and pay John for his new mode of transportation, John has gone by to pick up Carol (like old times, he thought, that's what this feels like), and Phillip and Janet and Melanie, all their belongings packed up in Janet's Accord, have stopped by before beginning the drive home. They slide three tables together to fit everyone in, and so it is 1989 now and everybody's made it through another year and now sit at a table in survivor mode grinning at each other like nothing has happened and nothing much has changed.

Dino's likes piping in Italian singers over the speakers to try and make the place authentic even without the presence of Italian food, so for now Vic Damone is crooning out 'Arrivederci Roma' while everyone pours ketchup on their French fries.

"We're not staying long," Phillip is saying. "I've got to be back in my office bright and early tomorrow morning and try to get some kind of plan going for my classes this semester."

"History doesn't change, dude," David says. "Just teach the same old thing you always have. Don't try to change everything to make it relevant. Don't try to give things a new perspective. Fuck perspective!" He looks at Janet and Melanie and Carol across from him. "Whoops. Sorry, girls. Haven't quite woke up yet. I'm not used to anybody civilized being around listening to me."

"I do it for me more than anyone else," Phillip says, "so I don't get bored and set in my ways too much. You're probably right, though. Half of them aren't listening anyway."

"You're all right, buddy," John tells him. "You're doing what you've always wanted to do. You're an inspiration. That's why I'm going in to work tomorrow morning and giving good old McGinnis Power my two-week notice. You folks are going to look at me funny when I say this, but here goes anyway. I've come to the realization that money isn't everything. I may be dead wrong, but I've been thinking for a while how I'm pushing forty and maybe it's about time I did something I like for a change. Or at least living somewhere I want to while I'm slaving to etch out a living. At least that way part of the day might be the least bit tolerable."

"You're just going to quit a good job? Just like that?" David looks at John like he is from another dimension.

"Sure," John says. "Isn't that what you did?"

"Oh, yeah," David grins. "I forgot that part."

"Go to the new store tomorrow," Sammy says. "They'll hire you back in a second. They're already hurting for help and they ain't even opened yet." "Sounds good," David says. He takes a sip of beer. He is the only one drinking. This is weird, he thinks. Up until a few days ago it has always been the other way around.

"I might just show up in a few days too." John looks at Miller and Sammy. "I don't know how long it's going to take me to find a job once I get back here for good. Who knows, I might even like working in a store again."

"Come on, then." Sammy says. "The more the merrier."

"At least your rent will be free," Carol smiles. "Utilities too."

"Carol's taking on a roommate," John grins. "Some girls never learn."

Phillip makes himself wait a polite fifteen minutes. He swallows down a hot dog and sips on a Coke, waiting to make sure Janet and Melanie are through eating before he starts boxing up their leftovers. All the time he is thinking of the proper way to say goodbye without anybody detecting how much he really means it.

(It's like this. It's like there is just so much you can say to anyone, no matter how close you are and how much you've all been through together. It gets to a point where it doesn't matter how far back you all go, because it's not any of that anymore, it's where you are now, and if you're not in the same place at the same time feeling the same sort of intimations, well then, it's all over, there's not that much to talk about

anymore, not that much worth sharing, you're too far apart, and the longer you take accepting the way it is the more difficult it makes it to move on and get to where you need to be. And it's not like all of this is final, you know, not any of this disappearing off into the sunset with the music swelling never to be seen again shit, no, it's not all that completely, because we'll all of us be back together again one of these days, I'll be back sometime, this is not forever by any means.

Except for some of it. Some of me and some of what's around me won't be back. Known it for a while now and that's just the way it is. Part of me and some of everyone else is gone for good.)

He shakes hands and pats backs, picks up his doggy box before he has to start hugging anyone, and lifts his hand. It's a smooth goodbye and they're out the door.

David really doesn't want to admit it, but the two beers he's quaffed down are making him feel like throwing up again. He's going to have to watch this or he's going to have a reputation for depositing his guts at the drop of a hat, so it's probably a good idea to follow in Phillip's steps and get home before anything embarrassing happens. He's a beginner at this, he thinks, it might be a good idea to slow down a little from this torrid pace he's been setting like a race horse these last few days. It's not like he's experienced or anything. It's not like he's been a wild man his entire life.

He leaves cash for his portion of the bill and says so long. He is happy with himself for being tough enough to make it out of the lot and around the corner to the edge of the Bank of America parking lot, where it's closed today, where he can get over to the side of the drive-thru and barf until the cows come home.

Hov'ring there
I've chased the shouting wind along, and flung
My eager craft through footless halls of air...

If he wasn't so sick to his stomach he could die laughing right now.

"I'm going to head out too," John says. "I need to take Carol back and get on the road. Seven A.M. comes early in the morning. But I'll see everybody real soon. It's not going to be too long."

There's a part of him that just wants to go home with Carol and not leave, just move in right now and start living his new-found life again, say to hell with his job and his existence back in McGinnis and never go back, but he knows that's not the way it works in the real world. He knows he has to get back and tie everything up, else this new abrupt stab at happiness may not come to be. He's thrown caution to the wind too many times before in this his one and only life; he needs to be careful and get it right this go-around. He's getting old and may not get that many more chances.

He takes Carol home and hits the highway, listening to the radio and giving himself lectures on how to not be a fuckup. He is doing his best to pay attention this time to what is being said, to finally get everything good and straight in his head.

***

Wednesday is the day when the store starts coming down, wrecking balls and machines of destruction and all that stuff. There have been two days of everybody in creation going in and out of the front doors and backing trucks into the wells at the back dock and loading up and hauling away anything that wasn't bolted down, shelving and fixtures and compressors and such. Sammy, being sidelined by his arm, and Miller, who refuses to lend any kind of physical hand to the proceedings whatsoever, observe all this activity sitting in the stripped to the bone front office, drinking coffee from a thermos and talking about how this panorama going on before and around them is about the sorriest sight either of them have ever seen

When the store's contents are finally stripped away and the cranes and bulldozers show up (mid-morning, so there won't be any problem with the rush hour), Miller and Sammy go and sit in lawn chairs on the grass out by Clement Avenue so they can watch the building come down. These are the same lawn chairs, Miller points out to Sammy, that they used to employ back in the long-ago summer nights after work when they would get out of their sucks at the back of the building, sitting by the dumpsters all hidden away from the world. They've been stored away in the backroom all these years, waiting for the time when they have the chance to return to their former glory.

"It just goes to show how they don't make quality products anymore like they used to," Miller says. "These damn chairs are about as old as us."

"That's pretty ancient," Sammy agrees.

"The only difference is these chairs still serve some kind of purpose. I can't say that much for you and me."

The process is no better than what they thought it would be. The crane swings a ball and plaster and brick fall and crumble, somebody sets off a charge of dynamite and the roof caves in, bulldozers come in and scoop rubble up and move debris around. By the time the crew is ready to eat lunch there's a long flat place where the Market used to be, and Miller and Sammy fold up their chairs and lay them down in the grass for the elements to consume. They won't be needing them again.

They've seen enough.

"Well, I've got to go get the rest of my damn training in," Sammy says. "I've put it off for as long as I can, but opening day is Friday, so it's either today or tomorrow."

"Have a wonderful time, buddy."

"You're going to have to break down and finish yours too, Miller. You may as well bite the damn bullet and come on and go do it with me right now."

"You can forget that part, Sammy. Because I'm not going. I'm not going to need any more training for my next gig."

This is said flatly, stated as fact, and Sammy can tell there's something going on here he needs to look a little further into and consider.

"What the hell does that mean?" he asks.

"It means, old pal, old amigo, that I'm not about to go get trained to do something I'm never going to do."

"I guess I'm not following you."

"I'm done, Sammy. I'm quitting Overton's and I'm quitting today. I've known I was going to walk away for a while now, but this is the first time I've actually said it out loud for anybody to hear. You're the only one so far who knows my master plan."

"Hell, Miller, you can't quit just like that."

"Watch me."

They walk to the new store where they've parked their cars away from the wreckage and debris and look at how the new lot is crowded with employee vehicles and vendor company cars and big and small trucks. From fifty yards off they stand and take in the gleaming structure standing there before them.

"All it took for me was one trip inside that place and I knew it was over," Miller says. "I knew I didn't want any part of it. Hell, Sammy, the way things are with me right now I don't even want to be in the same town as a new Overton's, much less work in one. That includes screwing around with Laurel too. And Jim and Abington and the whole nine yards. Everything."

"If it's Jim you're worrying about, forget it. He thinks I'm the one who's been slipping it to Laurel all this time."

"That's what I mean, man. How in the name of god can I go work at a place and have a boss who's fucking stupid enough to think his wife would prefer you over me?"They laugh over this, snort air through their noses, then Miller shakes his head."No, Sammy, I mean it. I'm through with the whole scene. I'm done, brother. Cooked. No rare or medium-well or anything like that, nope. I'm so well-done I'm charred. I've got to go somewhere different and do something else now before I get too damned crazy and old to make a change. I let a goddamn place like this get a hold of me one more time and I'll never get out." He looks at Sammy and smiles. "You know how it is with me, Samuel. I've been looking for something chock full of magic my whole life. If I don't go searching for my pot of gold at the end of the rainbow pretty soon I'll be too damned old to have time to look anymore."

"Go where? Do what? What do you have in mind?"

"Beats me. I'll try and figure it out."

"What are you going to do about your damn house? You can't just leave your fucking house behind. You're going to have to sell it before you can do anything."

"That's where you come in, brother. You've been talking about buying a house for about a thousand years now, so here's your chance. I'll make you a damn good deal on the place. You can say yes and move your ass in tomorrow and pay me what and when you can—I don't care. You'll never get a better bargain than what I'm giving you. The only thing is you have to promise to put me up any time I come back to the old hometown for a little visit. Don't start telling me I have to go find a frigging Holiday Inn and bed down there."

"So you're just going to quit your job, sell your house to me, and drive off in the goddamn Sun Bug to parts unknown, huh?"

"Why the hell not? Sounds like a good plan, even if it is me who came up with it. I'll load up all my books and clothes, say sayonara to the folks, and then maybe head to St. Louis and visit my sister, see what's happening out that way. They've got grocery stores in Missouri too, you know. I can work all day and go and see the Cardinals at night. Get drunk and fall out of the bleachers and get hauled away in a hearse on ESPN for everybody to see. That'll be special." He smiles at Sammy again. "Hell, Sammy, I can envision you as a rich landowner already. Manicured lawn, deck in the back, big privacy fence around the property. Shiny Corvette parked in the drive. The combination of that will get you more women than you can shake your Louisville Slugger at."

"I got enough women already. That's one reason I stay fucked up so much."Sammy acts like he's giving up and walks toward the store, stops in mid-stride and does an about face, then walks back to where Miller's getting in the Sun Bug.

"You're not bullshitting me, are you?" he asks, serious as a coronary thrombosis. "You're really thinking about going through with this?"

"When you gotta go, buddy," Miller tells him, "you gotta go. And nobody has noticed—not even me up until the last couple of days—but I've been in the act of checking out for a while now."

He starts the Sun Bug and drives over to the end of the lot where there's nothing much to look at, no old store standing there anymore for him to view. He gets out anyway and walks along the perimeter of where he remembers things used to be, the checkout lanes, the frozen food aisle, the meat department. Back there, he thinks, is where we sat at night after work, drinking and laughing, spinning our tales and shooting the shit. He thinks of how everybody had their silly dreams, how they all believed there was something waiting for them out in the world somewhere, in Abington, in another town or state, down the road and over the rainbow. He looks at where they'd gathered those times and sees how there is nothing there now. There is not even a whole uncrumbled solid brick left lying around to take away as a keepsake.

He looks closely through the rubble and the dust and tries to imagine himself once being present in this place, some ghost version of himself, another Bill. He does his best to recall what he'd said or what he'd heard, and even though he sees himself in the mirror each morning when he shaves it is hard now, impossible, to see the boy of long ago and the man of today ever occupying this place in any other facet but a dream. That is what it's been, he thinks, a dream. A guy can't live in a dream. It just doesn't work. Sooner or later he has to give it up.

So maybe he is a father and maybe he isn't. Unless he sticks around forever to see the kid grow up and perhaps look exactly like him he guesses he will never really know. Whatever is between him and Laurel will never go further than what it is today in this new year, which is nowhere, which is the fact that the love they shared was never really there anywhere truly but in his head, his sad romantic notion that he had to have tag along to justify this thing he was doing, what he was thinking, what he was teaching himself to believe to make it where he was not a bad person, not one of those void presences parading around out in the dark cold world. He stands now with the new Overton's over his shoulder, what's left of the old one before him, and he doesn't know what any of it ever really meant or means or if it matters one way or the other.

It wasn't love all this time. It isn't love today and never will be. You can't just give something a name and think that's what it is going to always be from that moment forward. It was never here long and it would never come to this same place again. He would have to look for it somewhere else, keep holding the damn fool belief in his head of how everybody gets lucky every now and then, how somehow it all works out in the end.

Even for him.

He looks around for a while, kicks at the rubble with his shoes. It is like he is trying to remember something for later that will tell him what he needs to know. He tells himself how maybe it will come to him one of these days or nights, and then it will all be straight in his head.

***

Sammy is inside the new Overton's for two hours. Despite everything modern and shining around him, it is not like there is that much more for him to learn, and he has spent most of this time watching people ambulating back and forth, walking somewhere to do something, twisting and turning and bending like they are in some big hurry to accomplish something unknown. He leaves and goes out the door to walk to his Corvette, and when he looks at where old Overton's once stood he sees Miller driving the Sun Bug away from it and out of the lot, taking a right on Clement Avenue, motoring on down the road and disappearing into the twilight.

www.ingramcontent.com/pod-product-compliance
Lightning Source LLC
Chambersburg PA
CBHW020916160726
47993CB00005B/2001